C000155989

THE ADVENTURES OF LOTTIE

Not All Bookworms Read

by Gill Meredith

Disclaimer

This is a work of fiction. Unless otherwise indicated, all the names, characters, businesses and incidents in this book are either the product of the author's imagination or used in a fictitious manner. Any resemblance to actual persons, living or dead, or actual events is purely coincidental.

Contents

CHAPTER ONE
THE AWAKENING

It was a Saturday morning and Lottie was window-shopping along Avignon's busy main road, the Rue de la République. She was loving her new life in the South of France with its azure blue skies and beautiful architecture. She wasn't deterred by the challenge of a new language or a different culture and embraced them both wholeheartedly as she reflected on how her life had changed in the last few months. It took several minutes for her to realise that she was being followed as she checked if the man who had crossed the road with her might continue down towards the city's outer walls or cross over the road to join her. Unfortunately, he blatantly opted to follow her and Lottie started to consider whether she might be in danger.

She had caught sight of his reflection in Monoprix's window and had stifled putting a hand to her mouth in alarm and instead had hurried into a luxury bag shop further along the road. The prices were well out of her range by several hundred euros so she had no idea how to react when an immaculately coiffured and expensively dressed woman approached her asking how she could be of assistance. Lottie weakly replied "*je ne fais que regarder*" causing the woman to smile politely with icy cold eyes that recognised she had another window shopper; a tourist who admired but never bought. Lottie was trying to decide if it might be a chance meeting, but he was now standing across the road and staring at the shop which rather declared she was his target. After picking up one or two of the leather bags and appearing interested, she decided that she didn't want to get trapped and exited the shop heading off down the street again sensing her pursuer was also crossing the road to take up his position behind her. She continued her stop-start perusal of the shop windows as her fuddled brain scrambled to build an escape plan to avoid him.

Realising that the busy shops were about to end and would become restaurants, bars and a public garden, she decided to cross over the road near the Tourist Office and walk back up towards the main square. She tried to walk casually even though her legs now felt like two lead bars and she'd given up hope of blending in with the shoppers. She repeatedly told herself "Do not look round, do **not** get eye contact". Lottie tried to linger in front of the windows given she had been enjoying herself up to the point that she'd seen him. The last time she'd seen that face was on the CCTV cameras at the *brocante* and she knew him as Jean-Louis Pislait; an aggressive and threatening individual.

There were times when he seemed to be gaining on her and there were only a handful of people between Lottie and her pursuer. It was only when she stopped and looked in the window of the BNP Paribas bank that she also became aware of a monk following behind Pislait. He stood out because of his black habit and a cowl that he had up over his head on such a warm, sunny day. She realised she'd seen him behind Jean-Louis from the onset but surely the monk had not walked down the road only to cross over and now come back up the same way? It seemed too much of a coincidence that they would all be taking this circuitous route. In the window's reflection she could see the monk was talking on a mobile phone; so much for renouncing all worldly goods she thought.

Lottie went into FNAC, a bookshop which also sold electrical goods. She went to the back of the store in the desperate hope that she had an overly fertile imagination which was creating this sense of fear. "Leave me alone" she muttered to herself as she saw Jean-Louis looking through books displayed on a centre table and even the monk was now in the store behind a display of i-pods and MP3 players. Suddenly, Pislait called out in English "Madame, I must talk to you" and she could see he was starting to make his way down the shop towards her. She weaved through the displays quickly edging her way to the front of the store and the pavement full of shoppers. Once outside, she gulped in the reassuring, fresh air as she considered her next move. Lottie realised she was perspiring and she could hear her heart beating somewhere up in her throat. She studied the crowds searching for the tell-tale blue polo shirt and navy trousers of a *Police Municipale* officer but there were none to be seen. If she could just get up to the square, then she'd be sure of finding one of the police officers carrying out the cat and mouse game of removing the beggars.

She could sense Jean-Louis upping his pace and there was only a smattering of shoppers between the two of them. She pressed on disregarding any further need to saunter and was now breaking into a jog. He was tall with long legs so every one of his strides would be two or three paces for her and she realised it was inevitable that he'd catch up with her. She reached in her bag for her mobile phone trying to remember if emergency calls were 110 or 112. She was five minutes from the square and she could see the multi-coloured, plastic canopies above the outdoor

3

restaurants when she heard him shout "Madame Pearce, please stop! It is very important I speak to you immed......" She disregarded his pleading tone as she was sure it would be another threatening exchange about the books. His words were broken by a screech of brakes and cries of alarm from several fellow pedestrians. She turned to face the commotion and was enormously relieved to see no sign of Jean-Louis or even the monk. With any immediate threat seemingly avoided, she walked back to a crowd of people standing around a large truck loaded with cement breeze blocks. She moved to the pavement edge to try and see around the mass of people who were all staring at the road in shock, some of them were already on their mobiles ringing for help and some were curiously taking photographs. The driver had jumped down from the truck and was ashen faced as he looked down at the man under his rear wheels. Lottie cried out in alarm as she saw the crushed torso of Jean-Louis trapped under the wheels. His eyes bulged in alarm and blood had started to drip on the road from the corner of his mouth. It was clear he would not be following her again and she found herself looking around for the monk but he was nowhere in sight. He'd vanished into thin air.

She walked solemnly towards the main square trying to make sense of the accident and found herself wondering if the monk was in anyway involved in Jean-Louis' demise. The general hubbub of pedestrian chatter and the screech and noise of the traffic were momentarily silenced as the sirens of two approaching police cars cut through the morning air. This was quickly followed by the blue flashing lights of a *pompier's* transit van as the fire brigade sped up the road to support the police in responding to an accident involving a member of the public. Lottie was now shaking from the drop in adrenalin and decided she needed alcohol.

4

She crossed the street to a welcoming bar where she fell into one of the rattan chairs and sighed long and hard. Fortunately, a lanky lad in a smart, black apron with the café's logo appeared within seconds and she ordered a dry, white wine and sat back to consider all the possible scenarios of how Jean-Louis had ended up under the truck. She knocked back the wine far too quickly even though she wasn't ready to leave her pavement retreat and was forced to order another glass; this time she warned herself to drink it more slowly. She reached for her phone as she needed to speak to someone and maybe Philippe could offer her advice. He was delighted to hear from her, but this quickly dissipated once she explained the morning's events. He told her she should go to the police station to report everything that she knew up to the accident. She challenged him wondering if it was just an accident even though she didn't believe Jean-Louis had slipped off the pavement at the same time as the truck had passed. Had the monk been behind him? Was the monk following Jean-Louis? Her head was spinning trying to decode the genuine fear that she'd felt from being shadowed by her two pursuers. When Philippe realised that Lottie's nerves were too shredded to take any appropriate action, he told her to give him the name of the café and he'd be there in a half hour.

Lottie was more than relieved when Philippe pitched up in front of her. She hauled herself wearily out of the chair for the customary "*bises*". He kissed her three times but then took her in his arms and hugged her solidly. Lottie could feel her chin drop and her mouth began to tremble. She told herself not to cry but it felt so great to have a man's arms around her again. It had been such a long time and she'd been through so much stress during the last few months. To her total embarrassment, she started to blub which only made Philippe search for a clean hankie in his various pockets whilst instructing the passing waiter to bring him a *noisette,* the French version of an espresso. He sat next to Lottie with one arm around her and one hand holding hers as, inch by inch, she detailed exactly what had occurred. Once she had finished, he gulped the coffee down in one hit and stood up announcing "*Ca suffit! Nous allons au flic*". After he'd paid, they swung left out of the café and headed on foot towards the Town Hall which housed the Police station.

Philippe took charge summarising the events in a brief conversation with the stony-faced agent who eventually realised the matter was more serious than first anticipated. He picked up a form and started to complete the various sections causing Lottie to search her bag for her passport as a valid proof of identity; thank God she always kept it with her. They were told to take a seat in the reception area adorned with pamphlets pronouncing the consequences of drugs, alcohol and crimes against homeowners and mainland France. Lottie shivered as the shock took hold again and Philippe wrapped a comforting arm around her shoulder once more.

They waited an eternity. Lottie, head bowed in fatigue, was beginning to wonder if it was all worth it when suddenly she found herself staring directly at the black boots of woman in front of her. She cast her eyes upwards to find a tall woman in fitted navy trousers with the obligatory pale blue polo shirt. She introduced herself as Brigadier-Chef Lepireon. Lottie only heard "*le pire*" and wondered if she had a nickname as the French words "*le pire*" translated as "the worst" in English. Her name seemed to lend itself to a wide range of monikers. She asked them both to accompany her to an office where she commenced the interview by data entering Lottie's details once more on her computer screen. Thankfully, she set off typing at a rapid pace as one of her colleagues at the adjacent desk appeared to be using just two fingers and stopping intermittently to refer to his notes. She didn't know his status, however, she felt extremely grateful to have the accomplished typist of the duo. On conclusion of the personal data, she started to pose a number of questions which Lottie sensed were being demanded by the software on her screen. She tried to answer them, but the questions didn't fit the events and she asked if she could just explain the last few weeks and then Madame Lepireon could enter the information. Philippe apologised and explained to Lottie that she should refer to her as *Brigadier-Chef or Madame L'agent* rather than "Madame" causing Lottie to redden and apologise profusely to the woman who'd only winced slightly at her loss of rank and status.

When Lottie reached the point of being followed by the monk, and the demise of Jean-Louis, she could tell Lepireon's interest had peaked. She asked more about the monk and took specific details of exactly where Lottie was in Rue de la République when she heard the noise of the lorry braking. Philippe and Lottie wondered if she'd be reviewing the street CCTV cameras after they'd finished the interview. Not for the first time, she wondered if she'd imagined being followed but there was no escaping the fact that Jean-Louis, a person she had not known some weeks ago, had threatened her and probably broken into the brocante. He was now dead and some poor lorry driver would probably lose his job and never be the same again.

Lottie thanked Brigadier-Chef Lepireon for recording the events and signed the various copies of her report. She'd read the document studiously worrying that her French wasn't up to it and that she was delaying the woman and Philippe. She was given a copy of the report and they were escorted back to the front reception area. There was no reference to "being in touch" as Lottie and Philippe considered the matter reported and, therefore, closed. They might have been a little more anxious if they heard Brigadier-Chef Lepireon instruct her hesitant typist colleague to pull all CCTV from Rue de la République and to get a team of Brigadiers to immediately request footage from the various shops.

Once outside, Lottie commented on the clinical and efficient manner of Brigadier-Chef Lepireon. She decided the woman's name was far too longwinded to reference every time and determined to nickname her "worst case". Against vehement protestations, Philippe advised he would ring her later to check she was alright and she was to try and relax and focus on the rest of the weekend. "C'est fini. Il y a rien à faire, ma chère Lottie" he declared reassuringly as the matter was indeed closed and there was no more that they could do. She wondered if he knew more than he was telling her as he seemed very certain and decisive. Lottie was still worrying about the monk who had disappeared but Philippe reiterated "c'est fini Lottie". She wandered back to the car with a sinking feeling that she was even starting to question the very people looking out for her. Was Philippe's insistence based on some knowledge of the event or simply that the matter was reported and out of their hands?

Later that evening, she lay in bed reliving the horrific death, the visit to the police station, and Philippe's generous assistance; both physically and emotionally. She thought about Bob, the funeral and everything that had happened since that day and she began to doubt herself. A sinking feeling crept over her that she'd made an unwise choice and, as much as she loved France, was it possible she had still been grieving when she opted to move here? Was it nothing more than the result of a rash and grief-stricken widow? She thought back to the funeral and the kitchen packed with people as she drifted into a half sleep and, suddenly, she was back in the old kitchen on the day of Bob's funeral.

She could hear Celia shouting "Do you want the crusts left on or cut off?" as her friend stood in front of a kitchen unit with several loaves of sliced bread and a stack of filled sandwiches in front of her like blocks of edible apartments. There was no reply from the sitting room because Lottie was fiddling with a bowl on the window ledge that served no purpose other than to hold the presents from old Christmas crackers throughout the years. No one ever felt happy to throw these tiny gifts away after the dining table was cleared and they sat in this silly bowl gathering dust. What use was a paper tape measure or a steel puzzle of 3 rings or some plastic fish that was able to tell if you were happy or sad? Lottie didn't need the fish to tell her how she felt. She had heard Celia but had chosen not to respond resulting in her friend shouting again with a tone of voice that recognised Lottie was only in the next room.

"Oh God!" she thought entering the kitchen taking in the group of close friends and one of her daughters, Elouise, all buzzing around doing "stuff". I don't want to be here she thought to herself deciding it would be far easier to walk away and maybe go for a stroll along the river with Bob. She reminded herself that he was no longer here and would never go for a walk with her again; well not in a physical sense. He'd disappeared from her life after thirty-four years of marriage. She was particularly angry with him as she'd been telling him for months that the apartment project was a step too far. Now the massive heart attack just proved what she'd been telling him time and time again, but Bob had always insisted that she was nagging and that he felt "fine". He had never listened to her voice of reason as there was always another jewel of a decrepit house to buy, renovate and sell on. When he turned the last one into apartments and decided to manage the rentals himself, his wife instinctively knew he was piling on a workload that would not end well.

No, Bob was not here and her family and dear friends needed her cooperation throughout the whole rigmarole of the funeral. Elouise, nicknamed Lou, came over and gave her mother a hug. As the eldest child, she could read her like a book and she knew exactly what her Mum was thinking. Lou had been up since six o'clock as she'd prepared and delivered all the flowers to the crematorium which had helped her florist's business and she hoped would demonstrate to family and friends just how gifted she was. Lottie smiled at her daughter in a conspiratorial manner recognising the rock she had been to her in the last few days. At last, her daughter was in a supportive and loving relationship with Martin, the local garden centre owner; he seemed a decent and caring man. The florist's shop had been instrumental in bringing them together as she had called into the nursery in a last-minute search of lily of the valley flowers for a wedding bouquet. Martin had taken personal responsibility to resolve her problem and they'd bonded from the minute they'd met. Lottie wondered whether her daughter's future would be secure at last as Martin clearly adored her, but would he pop the question any time soon? She certainly hoped so as Lou deserved some good luck after all her struggles as a teenage mother bringing up her son, Jake, on her own.

Thomas, her middle child, had agreed to do a small reading and was on route to Marlow from his house in Cornwall. She would be relieved when he arrived as it was a long journey to make on his own. The immediate shock had worn off and yet, as Lottie's only son, she was sure he felt the emotional weight of the whole family upon him. The kids had been hit hard by their father's unexpected death, but Lottie could take comfort that Lou was in a happy place with Martin, Tom was happy with his second wife, and her youngest daughter, Alison, continued to fly high in the city. They were all in good jobs even though Lou had known tough times having Jake at 18 when she was just a baby herself.

Thomas had a lot on his mind as he drove the many hours from Fowey in Cornwall. His wife, Isabella, had undergone several rounds of IVF and the last transplant appeared to be successful. She was only three months down a long road and he prayed they would have their own child to complete the family. The kids by his first marriage were both well balanced and delighted for their dad and Izzie. The house overlooking the river in Fowey was certainly large enough to absorb a number of children and Tom's job working for "Elegance", the yacht manufacturer, seemed to be going from strength to strength. He worked long hours causing the sales to roll in from around the world and he clearly loved his job. Lottie paced the floor hoping he would arrive soon so it would be one less worry for her frazzled nerves.

She did her best to engage with the mix of friends clogging up her kitchen. Bob's golf chums, Smithie and Frank, looked awkward and uncomfortable. She knew they felt like spare parts amongst the fussing women even though

11

Smithie was a terrific chef and could "hold his own" in the kitchen. Deborah, Bob's sister, asked the troops if they wanted a cup of tea and got a variety of responses. She had something to do as she set about gathering up the mugs and making yet another round of hot drinks since her arrival last night. Debs was every inch the spinster with her 1980s clothes, ornate jewellery and choice of excessive make-up. Behind the "slap" was a pretty woman with ginger hair even though she still insisted in perming it every few months. She'd been very close to Bob and Lottie knew that Debs needed to be busy otherwise she would crumble and cry. Lottie was on a knife-edge herself and they weren't even at the crematorium yet.

Lottie's own brother, Alex, had been the dependable rock that she knew he would be. He'd arranged the appointment next week at the solicitor's office even though he had his own practice in High Wycombe. The family links made it convoluted to use him when they'd bought the house, so they'd opted for a local practice and then just carried on using them over the years. Just as Lottie was lifting the mug of tea, the doorbell went heralding the arrival of Thomas as he threw his keys onto the hall table and scooped her up in his arms. She didn't know if she wanted to scream, cry, shout, or slide to the floor and let someone take responsibility for her. She hugged him and then pushed him away to take in his appearance. He normally had his black hair slightly longer and a bit floppy around the front but today it was cut short and he looked a bit odd and far too polished. Lottie appreciated the hair cut was probably a sign of respect to his dad, so she buttoned the comment about to leave her lips and smiled affectionately as she ruffled it slightly. He went through to the kitchen to grab a tea and a bite to eat.

The doorbell chimed again and Lottie headed off to find the last of her brood had arrived. Alison looked immaculate in a navy suit and cream blouse with her blond hair swept up in a messy chignon. She looked vulnerable and cute even with red-rimmed, puffy eyes as she hugged her mother enthusiastically. Alison popped into the kitchen to say "hello" to her brother, sister, and the assorted friends.

Lottie was now in a deep sleep and the memories shifted from the kitchen to the reading of her husband's Will and the metamorphic shock that awaited her. She had insisted the children didn't need to accompany her but Lou, being local, had stood firm and arrived to drive her to the solicitor's practice in Marlow. Lottie had a rough idea of the contents of the Will as they had bought some shares along the way when Bob's finances were in a healthy position and when there was spare cash available. Both the personal bank account and the business account were in good shape and the various properties had created nest eggs for them all. These savings and investments did not include the monthly rental fees even if the children eventually decided to sell the property. Lottie knew she didn't want the pressure of ensuring the flats were occupied or obtaining the rent each month. She knew Bob had one renter who hadn't paid for three months and was in the middle of legal letters trying to evict him. Look what the stress had done to him; she really didn't need the hassle.

Clive Hodgkins came out of his office exclaiming "Mrs Pearce, welcome, please come in, yes, please come in. Ah, I presume you're Elouise, my my how you've shot up. Yes, yes, please come in. My condolences that we meet under these circumstances. Do follow me, yes, do come in". They both followed him hoping he wasn't going to repeat everything twice which would be absolute torture and it would be hours before they could escape. They entered the inner sanctum of his wood panelled office in which towers of files were stacked behind him on a leather topped table; clearly these fixtures were seldom referenced. Lottie wondered how often he got to pick up one of them and how long clients had been waiting for a decision, a letter, or the outcome to their problem. Perhaps he wanted to look busy and yet the tottering tower of files created the opposite effect and the stacks just looked chaotic.

Clive Hodgkins was a curious figure who was probably in his early sixties and looked like a cross between a character from Gringotts' Bank in the Harry Potter films and someone who could have stepped out of a Charles Dickens' book. His three-piece black pinstripe suit and rimless glasses gave him a cold, detached appearance. Lottie acknowledged his further expression of condolence as he outlined the structure of the reading of her husband's Will. She was rather surprised when Hodgkins advised that Bob had left a letter to be read before he could disclose the contents of the Will. Lou frowned at Lottie inquisitively as she saw Hodgkins pass Lottie the envelope that had her Mum's name handwritten on it in her father's handwriting. Seeing her dad's spider-like scrawl caused tears to well in her eyes and she placed her hand on her mother's in a gesture of reassurance. It seemed an irregular start to an event which they were expecting would be straightforward.

Darling Lots   *March 1989*

How sensible you were to make me write a Will once the kids came along. I'd never have done it and I assume that something has caused my death. I can't think it is old age as we'd have prepared for that along the way and made changes to the Will to allow for grandchildren. Whatever

14

has happened, darling, I am so sorry to leave you and the children. I cannot imagine how my life would have been without you. I know that the various properties have helped our bank balance and the shares that we bought for the children will be their future. I don't know if I was retiring or still buying ~~recks~~ wrecks, but all the profits are for you, Tom, Lou and Ali. Ed will know how to release the funds from the business accounts. I hope you'll all get a decent income each month.

Now my Lots I need to tell you something that I have not told you before and it's ~~born~~ borne out of love and it's difficult to know where to start. When we first met, I fell in love with you immediately. I never wanted anything to threaten that love and I never told you something because I was scared that you'd leave me, not marry me, and we'd no longer be together. Now I realise that was a mistake because I am not with you when you read this and I can't hold you, let you hit me, let you shout. I was just scared Lottie and I need you to remember this.

When I was 19, you know that I took half a year out before starting work at Uncle Mat's construction business. It was an adventure with a couple of mates that took us to France where we drank beer until it came out of our ears and we drove the French girls crazy with our franglais and awful English accents. You know I went to France in 1983 but you don't know much more as it was a few years until we would meet each other at the club. During the time in France, I met a girl called Mireille and we were an item for a while. When I got back to the UK, she had my phone number at mum and dad's and she rang me. She was pregnant and she wanted to keep the baby. She didn't need me to be involved unless I wanted the baby, but some financial help would be appreciated. You know what an

15

idiot I was as a teenager and can you imagine how I would have coped being a dad at 19? OK, Lottie, are you still with me? I think you're probably feeling sick and angry that this remained hidden, but you must know that I was scared you'd run a mile if I told you. Within days of meeting you, I knew you were "the one" and I didn't want anything to come between us. I realise that I should have risked it, but I was too happy to tell you of the mess I'd made as a young 'un. You were always the sensible one and you didn't have any skeletons in your own cupboard.

Mireille (Mimi) had a daughter, Fleur, in 1984. I sent her 5000 euros a year via Hodgkins' office until Fleur was independent. She wouldn't take any more than that and it was easy to transfer the funds from the business account to her French bank without making any of this too visible. Darling, I have left her a few thousand pounds now to acknowledge my responsibility even though Fleur is all grown up and I know she works in Paris but I'm not sure where or what she does. Mireille was older than me as she was 21 but I have no idea when you will read this or what age she will be when you read my letter. I think she is still in Avignon. She was when I talked to her about our marriage in 1988 - the best day of my life.

Lottie, believe me that I adored you, adore you, and would not have done anything that would have caused you to leave me or not marry me. The solicitor knows how to contact Mireille and Fleur. Don't blame old Hodgkins. He was under instruction not to disclose this until you had been handed this letter. He will have had her address since we set up the arrangement and I know he will be certain of her whereabouts. Mireille knows that she will receive a gesture from me when I die. As I said, she never made demands on me and she is a good woman. I can't think you will meet her, but she knows all about you and how lucky I was to find you and that you loved me.

I will love you forever and I am sorry something has caused me to go and you have to stay. I will wait for you and for the moment I can take you in my arms again. I am sorry that this secret is no longer a secret and I'm even sorrier that I didn't trust telling you. I am an idiot, I remain an idiot, and you never deserved me. All my love to you and our gorgeous children. Your Bob xxxx

She got to the end of the letter and slumped in her chair. Ever so slowly and very quietly she uttered "Jesus Christ, you bastard". Lottie's mother would not be happy with her as she was anti-swearing saying that it just showed a lack of education. Lottie disregarded the mental reprimand as Bob clearly was a bastard to have kept such a secret and for thirty plus years. She looked at Hodgkins in an accusatory manner given he had played an active role in such deceit. Lou was pressing her to explain why she'd just called her father a bastard. She wondered if he'd left everything to a Builders' Accident Fund, the Cats Society, or some other unrelated recipient. All Lottie could do was pass her the letter to read and Lou exhaled long and hard as she came to the end of it. She covered her head in her hands muttering "Dad, how could you do this to us?"

Lottie realised she needed to get the meeting concluded as soon as possible and escape so she could sort out the hurricane whirling in her head. She asked Clive Hodgkins to read the Will which contained no other surprises other than a financial gesture to the woman with the daughter. Lottie and Lou fell out of the solicitor's practice. Lou was full of questions which poured out of her in a tumbling mess. They realised that they had no answers to the questions as the only person who knew the answers was Bob, the husband, the father, the secret keeper.

On the journey back home, Lottie rang Tom and Alison to confirm the contents of the Will and to advise they had a half-sister living in France. Both absorbed the information in silence although they subsequently reacted in different ways. Tom was angry and took to swearing down the phone which brought a few of his work colleagues to his office to check on him. Alison exhaled long and hard exclaiming "Good God, Mum, you really didn't know about any of this?" She was not as shocked as Tom but was extremely upset that her dad could be so duplicitous. They both needed time to take in the information and she hung up advising she'd call them later. Lottie couldn't decide if she should be more affronted that the children had an unknown sibling in the family or Bob's disloyalty to her.

Was she unreasonable or did she lack understanding? The last three weeks had been hell, but it seemed the hell was not over yet as she clutched his letter in her hands and resisted the urge to rip it into shreds. She looked at his handwriting and wondered if he had ever envisaged this moment and how she would feel or how his children would feel? As they approached the house and the shock was diminishing, Lottie realised that she had not asked for any details of this woman called Mireille or of her daughter, Fleur. She decided to ring Clive Hodgkins and get the information as she wanted to write to her or even send an email if he had an email address. Once Lou felt sure that her Mum was back on an even keel, she made her farewells and headed back to Martin's in Maidenhead. She needed his gentle reassurance that the world was not going mad and to hear him remind her that her dad was a good man. She would need to tell her son about the addition to the family unit, but the news would keep for the moment.

Smithie rang in the evening to ensure the meeting had gone without a hitch and to confirm that she could call into the office any time to go through the accounts. She was tempted to tell him of the letter but decided against it. Did he already know? She felt sure that Ed, the firm's accountant, would be aware of Mireille and her daughter as you couldn't move 5000 euros a year without questions being asked. Would she look at her friends from now on wondering if they were in on the deceit? She decided to ring Deborah and check if Bob's sister was up to speed. She could confirm that Bob had left her £20,000 and check that she had got home OK following the funeral. During the conversation, she casually dropped in a mention of Bob's trip to France as a student and waited. Debs seemed genuinely confused by the reference and asked if Lottie was going to take a holiday there or a perhaps a long weekend away following all the distress. Lottie confirmed that she might think about a few days' break and advised Hodgkins would be in touch as Probate had been a relatively quick process.

Lottie hung up the phone and rang Hodgkins' office. He was still there beavering away in the solitude of his office; no wife or children to demand his presence of an evening. Keeping her voice calm and measured, she asked him for Mireille's contact details and noted down her phone number, the postal address, and an email address. She couldn't bring herself to be anything other than business-like with him. He had supported them over the years, but she felt wounded by Bob's secret that had been maintained by him for so long. She sensed he was about to explain Bob's motivation in withholding the information, so she cut

19

him off abruptly by thanking him for the details and hanging up.

She looked at the phone number with so many more digits than her own and noted the unfamiliar email address; all of which smacked of a distant land. "Mireille Rivaud" she curled the name around her mouth and spoke it out loud. "Mireille Rivaud, Bob, why did you keep her a secret? Did you still hold feelings for her?" She thought back to the birth of Elouise and that he was already a father at that point. Even given her hormones at the time, had it really been so difficult to explain his past? Lou had given birth to Jake at eighteen which struck her as an even better time to explain about his own child at nineteen. Had he seen Fleur and Mireille since the birth? She reflected on one or two golfing holidays with Smithie and Frank which had been in France. Were they down in the south even though they'd said they were going to the northern coastal resort of Wimereux? How many times had he lied over the years and was it easy to lie to her? "Stop, for God's sake STOP!" she exclaimed out loud. Lottie realised she would drive herself insane with all the unanswered questions. She erased the doubts by confirming the past was exactly that – a life already behind her and Bob and it could not be changed, no matter how painful it might be. Nothing good came from regretting history so she decided that it would be better to focus on the present and to consider her future and her children's future. Yes, that was the way forward and she would ask the children to view it the same way so that discussions of Mireille and her daughter could be kept to a minimum.

She kept the bit of paper with Mireille's details behind the box of matches on the ledge above the fireplace. She looked over at it from time to time and thought about how she would contact her. Eventually, and when her resentment had dissipated for the woman, she decided the moment had arrived and she would write an email to her. It would have to be in English and she hoped the woman would be able to understand it even though she had learned French for a while and had used it at the antique shop where she still worked two afternoons a week. There were two dealers in Paris who rang from time to time asking for certain English items of furniture for wealthy clients. She enjoyed using her French particularly as the phrase "use it or lose it" was certainly true when it came to a foreign language. The email would take quite a long time to compose, and she might want to change it, so she put in her own address. There had been various moments when she'd put in someone's email address only for the communication to go flying off half complete or not re-read. She needed an electronic brake on her words until she was ready for the email to be despatched. She sat in front of her laptop and started.

Dear Madame Rivaud
I am writing to you following the death of my husband
Robert Pearce (Bob). Before the reading of my husband's
Will, our solicitor gave me a letter written by him. In this
letter he explained about his relationship with you during his
holiday in the South of France when he was 19. I realise
this was long before Bob and I had met. I have just learned
that you had a child together and she is called Fleur. I am
assuming that Clive Hodgkins has advised you of Bob's
death and I apologise if I am telling you about this
information for the first time.

As you can imagine, I am in a state of disbelief that my
husband could keep this secret from me. I was also
unaware that he was such a good actor following his tears

at the birth of our first child, Elouise, when he was already a father. I am sure you recognise that Bob was a good man and he has left you a financial sum following his death. I am aware that he supported you both with an amount that you agreed at the time of the birth.

I have advised our three children (Elouise, Thomas and Alison) of their half-sister Fleur. I am sure they are also curious to know more about you and your daughter. Even though it has been a terrible shock and I am naturally angry that Bob kept this secret from me, I hope that we can communicate in the next few weeks to learn a bit more about each other. I am curious to see a photo of Fleur if you feel able to send one to us.
Regards
Charlotte Pearce

Lottie had made a number of amendments to the email having scrutinised every word for hidden meanings or a possible lack of understanding by the Frenchwoman. She kept the email in "draft" until the next morning when she sat down with a cup of coffee and looked at it again. It was neither cold nor overly friendly. It had the right tone of surprise which was how she felt but it kept a door open if Mireille wanted to write to her. She realised that she came across as a bit possessive of her husband but that mirrored exactly how she felt about this woman and her daughter who had suddenly appeared in their lives. She hit "send" and exhaled loudly feeling a slight sense of relief even though she was not sure why she should feel that way.

She pottered around the house in the morning until the time arrived for her to go to work in the antique shop in Marlow. She had been helping Barbara Radford-Jones a couple of afternoons a week for the past eighteen months and enjoyed a job that reminded her of her days as prop master at Henley Theatre. She had a good knowledge of period furniture and dressing props and was adequately trained to recognise items that were correct for the various periods of history. She'd received a couple of large reference volumes as Christmas presents from Bob over the years and Barbara also had a few books in the showroom. She enjoyed bringing her knowledge up to speed when there were no customers as antiques had always been an interest. The normality of returning to work felt wonderful and she sold an escritoire and a couple of carriage lamps before closing the shop having left a note for Barbara confirming she'd be back in Tuesday afternoon.

She returned home feeling elated by the sales and opted to celebrate the return of normality with a sirloin steak and a glass of claret. She rang the kids to update them on her day and told them she'd emailed Mireille which generated lengthy discussion as to whether she would get a reply. Tomorrow Lottie would be back in the charity shop in Marlow where she volunteered Wednesday and Friday mornings. The part-time work had been suggested by Bob who could sense that the empty-nest syndrome was starting to depress his wife. Lottie felt good to have a sense of purpose in the coming days even if nothing stopped her brain from whirring about Bob. She relieved certain memories of happy times but couldn't eradicate everything that had happened in the last few weeks. She'd spent many hours wondering how she could "join" Bob, but she recognised that she was turning a corner on those dark thoughts.

She'd sunk a half bottle of the claret when she decided to check email. The *in-box* contained a host of messages of condolence together with a few invitations from close friends but the one that stopped her in her tracks was headed "thank you" and alongside it she could see the name of Mireille Rivaud. She stared at it feeling scared and emotional. Why had she drunk half the wine when she would need her wits about her? She clicked on the mail and read:

Dear Mrs Pearce

Forgive my English. I am not to use it all the time. I have a brocante shop in Avignon and I have many tourists so I will use the English language sometimes.

You have no idea as happy I am to receive your email. I was told by Monsieur Hodgkins that Robert has gone. I am very sorry. He was very diligent in helping me and also Fleur. She is a lovely girl and you can see a photo that is joined in the email. She is happy and lives in Paris. She is in "La maison de Christian Dior" and I am the proud mother.

We must talk now as you are dear to contact me. I am pleased but I know this is a difficult time. Perhaps one day we can meet to talk of the father of Fleur and together of your children? Thank you for your letter to me. I value your gesture.

Yours sincerely
Mireille RIVAUD (Mimi)

Lottie read the message three times appreciating the effort that the woman had made to write to her in English. She looked at the attachment symbol alongside the note, inhaled deeply and clicked on it. In front of her was a pretty woman with aquiline features and long black hair with a silver strip running from the edge of her fringe down behind

her ear. She looked elegant and "classy". She searched
for Bob in the girl's features, but she could not really find
anything although maybe the shape of her chin resembled
Bob's. It surprised her that she was not looking at a mini-
Bob and she wondered whether this Mireille woman had
tricked him. Then she thought about their own three
children. Tom had many of Bob's mannerisms and his
snub nose but both Lou and Ali tended to look more like
her. It didn't really prove anything and she could hardly
have imagined a nineteen-year-old Bob pressing for DNA
proof, nor Neville or Margaret, his parents. She decided
that there was nothing in the email that she needed to hide
from the children, so she forwarded on Mireille's email and
photo adding a small note above it. She had decided she
would reply to her tomorrow.

The next day she got a call from Ed, the accountant
managing Bob's business, as he had a proposal for her to
consider. The company was in a state of flux following his
death and Ed and Clive had put their heads together and
decided they would like to take it over if she was in
agreement. Clive was a middle-aged friend of Bob's who
knew everything about the building trade which, combined
with Ed's invaluable experience as the bean counter, would
create a promising duo to continue the company. She
confirmed the proposal made sense and requested Ed draw
up a list of the assets and values which could be checked
by her brother. She gave Alex a call to alert him to Ed's
proposal noting the relief in his voice as he readily agreed
to check over the figures and ensure she received a correct
price.

Lottie was beginning to worry about the number of evenings
that were being spent watching the flat screen television.
She probably needed a hobby and she wondered if it was

were really financial security for the children as her needs were few and they were bringing up children of their own or would be if dear Isabella ultimately gave birth and Ali wasn't to remain a workaholic.

Lottie went to make a hot drink and had the mug of tea to her mouth when the handle completely came away dropping the china into the sink. Lottie burnt her hand as the liquid bounced back onto her skin and without any rhyme or reason she started to cry. The tears poured out of her and she found herself gasping between the sobs as she inhaled small gulps of air as the tears continued to fall. She sat on the kitchen stool and grabbed a couple of sheets of kitchen towel. She didn't really know why she was crying other than wondering if this was a very late reaction to the events of the previous weeks which has been building like a pressure cooker. Now with Bob's business almost sorted, it was like any memory of Bob was slipping out of her reach and everyone was "back to normal" around her. Was she alright? Would she know how to live a life without him? Eventually, Lottie's tears dried and she found that she actually felt a lot better. It was as if the pressure had cleared and the tension in her head and body had been released. She felt positive after weeks of being in an infinite maze of gloom.

She popped into the cloakroom to throw some cold water on her face and tidy her hair just in case anyone suddenly rang the doorbell. On returning to the kitchen, she pulled the flight information out of her handbag and opened up her laptop. She booked a flight giving her two nights in the city and decided she'd sort out a *chambre d'hôte* in the next few days; there must be loads of bed and breakfast places in or near Avignon. She pinged an email to Mimi with the dates and also sent a text message to Barbara who would be pleased that she was taking a break at the end of the month. She also sent a message to Celia who managed the charity shop so she could arrange cover.

Lottie couldn't help but smile as she closed the laptop and reflected on the surprising rapport that had developed between the two women. In the beginning, she'd reached out to Mimi to learn more about her which was an obvious reaction to the letter. Nothing had prepared Lottie for the woman's warm, friendly personality and the speed of their bond. What would Bob have made of it all?

CHAPTER TWO
SOUTH OF FRANCE

As she slept, Lottie eyelids twitched repeatedly as the story went through the many phases of the last few months. She was now lying horizontally across the bed as her brain recalled the first trip to Avignon. Mimi was suggesting she stay with her over the few days precipitating Lottie to politely refuse the thoughtful invitation. She wasn't sure she was ready for such intimacy as Bob's liaison still had the potential to be a fragile link between the two women and she didn't want to put a strain on their new relationship. She researched various *chambre d'hôte* establishments in the city centre and fell upon a decently priced room right near the Palais des Papes; a tourist hotspot that she'd read about when people mused of living in the South of France.

Lottie's brother, Alex, rang to advise the figures for the business and the amount offered was a good price if a little generous on the part of Ed and Clive. He envisaged no problem in Lottie relinquishing the business to them and, on her agreement, would prepare the documentation. Lottie confirmed to go ahead and made a mental note to check with the children about the flats and check whether anyone wanted to manage the rentals or if they would prefer to sell the building. She rang each of the kids in the evening to update them on the sale of the business. She had decided that every member of the family would get a quarter of the sum as she had no idea what might be around the corner for her and wanted to maintain a level of financial independence from the kids. She also asked each of them about managing the flats and the level of responsibility required in maintaining their upkeep and occupancy. Tom wasn't interested as he had enough on his plate, nor did Lou who held a similar view to Lottie that they could prove to be an administrative pain let alone the maintenance issues. Ali, however, did seem to be interested and asked to be given a bit of time to consider the pros and cons of further responsibilities. Lottie let her know about the current issues with one of the renters being three month's late in rental payments. It was vital to let her know what Bob had been going through before his death.

Mimi sent an email to Lottie in the evening suggesting another Skype call at the weekend. Lottie proposed Saturday afternoon as it was the car boot on the Sunday. She wasn't sure if Mimi would be working at the *brocante* but she had understood enough to know that she owned the building but a number of antique/bric-a-brac collectors shared their availability to oversee the customers visiting the premises. She thought she remembered Mimi saying she worked Mondays to Thursdays, someone else worked Fridays and Saturdays and the shop was closed, like most of France, on Sundays. She had only just sent a reply when she's received Mimi's confirmation that she'd call her at 17h00. She "Googled" the city of Avignon on her tablet and a selection of photos displayed winding lanes, some of them cobbled, and the city seemed a little suspended in history and in time. There was definitely a strong feeling of cultural identity which was so predominant in France.

By the time the Skype call came around, Lottie felt a little more in tune with Avignon and its various districts in the city. She asked where *the brocante* was located which was

not too far from the Palais des Papes and in a district called
Le Pontet. She had a long chat with Mimi about a whole
raft of subjects and found herself once more appreciating
this incredibly sensitive person who was so easy to talk to.
Unfortunately, Fleur's busy diary would prevent her
daughter from being available during Lottie's visit but they
could still hook up by phone or Skype during her mini break.
Inwardly, Lottie felt relieved as she was capable of meeting
Mimi during this first trip but to meet Fleur too might have
created an emotional "wobble" given Bob's recently
exposed secret.

It proved to be a very full weekend containing many
moments when she genuinely felt happy. Yes, she still
ached for Bob to walk through the kitchen door and throw
his car keys on the hall table but, little by little, she was
accepting this was not going to happen. She considered
how delighted he would have been to learn that his
youngest daughter would manage the apartments following
his death. He would be proud of her whilst Lottie could only
worry about the additional workload on top of her
daughter's demanding job.

It was two weeks later that Lottie found herself on the flight
to Avignon. Bob's business was in the process of being
sold, Ali had taken over the rental building and sharing
funds with her siblings, and Lottie was contemplating a life
without Bob. She was only 56 so, hopefully, had many
years ahead of her. She wasn't a natural talker on flights
and preferred to read a book or listen to music but her
neighbour next to the window had other plans. Her flight
companion was a woman returning to her home in Isle-sur-
le-Sorgue where she'd lived for nine years. She'd married
a Frenchman and carved out a new life with him having
been divorced at a young age. She was witty and

entertaining and in no time at all the plane was landing at "Avignon Provence Airport". It seemed only five minutes ago that it had taken off on a gloomy day with leaden skies. As the plane door opened, Lottie was hit by the strikingly blue and cloudless sky. According to the First Officer, the temperature was thirty-two degrees and Lottie hoped her jeans wouldn't prove to be too hot. She was glad she'd packed a pair of beige slacks in the carry-on.

She wished her neighbour a safe journey home and thanked her for the glowing insight into a life in France and for changing the 20 euros note into small denominations and some useful change. Once out of the airport, Lottie sought out a bus to the city centre and knew to look out for the gilded statue of St Mary that sat atop the Palais des Papes. She pressed her nose to the window to ensure she didn't miss her the tell-tale landmark. She decided to go straight to the *chambre d'hôte* called "*Les Fleurs d'Inès*" so she could settle herself in her room. It was years since she'd travelled on her own as holidays had always involved the whole family and she couldn't remember the last time she was abroad in just her own company. It was all very exciting and she reflected how thrilled she'd been to get the array of colourful euro notes prior to her departure.

Once she'd met Madame, who she presumed was called Inès, she unpacked her handful of toiletries and hung up the change of clothing. Lottie commended herself on her great choice of accommodation as the *chambre d'hôte* was clean, welcoming and in a perfect location tucked down a pretty side street away from the noisy square. Her potluck decision appeared to be awash with restaurants and bars and there would be plenty of choice this evening.

Lottie was excited at the possibility of exploring the city before meeting Mimi tomorrow and happily strolled around the shops beguiled by the display of foreign brands from the beautifully wrapped confectionery to the exquisite but expensive clothes. Window shopping was a favourite pastime and the enjoyment tripled when it was abroad. Lottie watched as a woman bought some flowers in a florist shop where the counter seemed practically on the pavement. The love with which the flowers were scooped up, the wrapping of the blooms in the palest pink tissue paper, then the plastic film wrapped around the tissue all took precious minutes which the patient buyer took in her stride. She stood silently accepting the respect given to the bouquet. Not content with the plastic and the tissue, next came a pink ribbon that was cut, curled, and wrapped around the stems, then a small twirl of pink was stuck to the plastic outer wrapping with the florist's business card. It was mesmerising and a spectacle in purchasing where the level of care far outweighed anything she'd seen in buying a bouquet in a florist's shop at home. She mentally recorded the end result as she'd tell Lou all about it when back home.

Lottie decided to do a tour of the Palais des Papes or Popes' Palace. She'd read a bit about the ancient residence when researching Avignon and it was a few hours later, after walking for ages and up and down stairs, that her early morning start began to catch up with her. It was a stunning building but she could sense her attention was beginning to lag as she thought of the evening stretching out ahead of her. She returned to the *chambre d'hôte* to have a quick nap to get a second wind before dining later in the evening. She sent a quick WhatsApp to Lou to let her know she was safely installed and asked her to update the others. Thank heavens she had selected a side street rather than the main square as there was only a slight buzz of pedestrians below her which did not prevent her nodding off. She woke a couple of hours later feeling refreshed and ready for a second round of exploration.

Lottie walked along the rows of restaurants that all merged with each other in the Place de l'Horloge. It seemed the only separation of ownership was a change in the colour of the chairs or the manner in which the tables were arranged. She had half an eye on the stands displaying the menus and half an eye on a beautiful carousel. Several children were clambering onto the array of horses or into the various seats in anticipation of it moving in the next few minutes. It had a tiny staircase that led to an upper level, so the more adventurous ones were clambering up to the top. All around her were the excited squeals of the children and the parents were laughing and taking photos of their chicks. Behind the carousel was the Hôtel de Ville or Town Hall where people were entering and departing like a constantly rotating swing door as they conducted their administrative affairs. Next to it was an equally impressive building in the form of the Opera Theatre, both splendid and classical edifices in their own right.

Lottie wandered the lanes looking for a restaurant away from the tourist area even though it would be a great choice for people-watching. She came across a much cheaper restaurant with bright yellow gingham tablecloths and a huge olive tree growing in the middle of the dining room. The tables were arranged around its majestic, gnarled trunk and a glass roof ensured there was sufficient daylight for this unusual feature. The tree had been cut into a saucer shape thereby ensuring no one was likely to get a sharp branch in their eye. The Mediterranean menu was appetising and atypical to the restaurants back home and it had a number of curious descriptions in French and

English, so she ventured inside. It was still early evening but she was more than happy to eat early and readily accepted an aperitif from her attentive hosts. She sipped on her gin and tonic and selected a tomato and mozzarella starter followed by a daube d'agneau with a selection of vegetables; she was rather pleased that she knew it was a lamb stew without the aid of a thoughtful translation. She opted for a glass of Côte du Rhône with her lamb main course which was beautifully tender and she wondered if it had been marinating for hours or perhaps days. She finished off the meal with a refreshing slice of Tarte au Citron but refused a coffee as she decided to have this back in the central square. It was a mild evening and she chose a bar with an open decked area arranged with small tables and chairs. She didn't wait long to find a space as Avignon seemed awash with couples and families so not many people sought a table for one. She tried to remember to adapt to the relaxed style but still found herself looking around after a few minutes to catch the eye of a passing waiter who had developed a skill in deliberately not making eye-contact. She ordered a café crème when the waiter eventually came to her taking a clutch of orders on route to her table and even more on the way back into the bar. She instructed herself to "chill" and settled down to watch the array of people in the square.

She studied the single people, the couples and the families wondering about their lives and what brought them into the centre of Avignon. How many were visiting and how many lived in this lively and friendly city? One or two city police seemed in evidence to move on the occasional drunk who tried to inveigle cash out of people; they clearly wanted a sanitised view of the city for the tourists. Lottie returned to her B&B once the evening light had disappeared and was greeted by Madame who asked her what sights she had visited and where she had eaten dinner. She tried to remember where she had eaten but had got rather lost in twisting and turning down the various lanes. In the end, her description of the olive tree was sufficient for Inès to declare "*Bravo! Un bon choix Madame Peas!*"

Lottie woke up refreshed and ready for the day ahead. She went into the breakfast room that had two tables still laid with a plethora of goodies and another where a couple had clearly already departed to maximise on their day in the city. She enjoyed the fresh pastries and was pouring over a bus timetable and map when Inès came back in the room to check if she had everything she needed. "*Madame, je dois aller à Le Pontet ce matin, il y a un car que je peux prendre?*" quizzed Lottie. Inès explained Le Pontet was a large commercial centre and there were a few buses outside the city walls that would head to the district: particularly the ones going to Vedène. Lottie thanked her and stepped out into the streets where the aroma of freshly ground coffee beans hung in the air as she passed the various eateries. She walked out of one of the large openings of the walled city and was alongside the fast-moving River Rhône shimmering in the morning sun.

It didn't take long to find a bus heading towards Vedène and she was soon settled alongside a woman and small child. The bus drove past a large tourist wheel which was erected between the river and the walls of Avignon. It seemed these monstrosities were everywhere, no matter the country or the city. Behind it were some stunning Viking River cruisers and she could only imagine the comfort and luxury of a trip that would sail into Avignon as one of its many destinations. They oozed money and she wondered what the average price of a week or two might be aboard these chic river boats.

It was tricky trying to spot where she was in relation to her map but she enjoyed walking and decided to get off twenty minutes later. She weaved her way through the streets until she arrived at a huge building with a large wrought iron sign swinging on its rusty hinges proudly exhibiting "*Les Antiquités de Mimi*". She could feel nerves setting in and her stomach seemed to have dropped to her feet sensing some sort of threat. Had she agreed too readily to this visit and would she regret her decision? There was no way back now even though her head was buzzing with images of Bob, Mireille, Fleur and her supportive kids.

She went through an archway into a small courtyard awash with colourful flowers and plants. They were hanging off the front of a rusty bicycle, tumbling from an old enamel bath and sitting in more traditional pots and urns. There were also several old doors and window frames resting against the bright, stone walls. It wasn't obvious how much of the architecture belonged to her friend although she could see the main entrance on the right-hand side. She stepped through the doorway and into a small reception area containing a desk piled high with papers and files. Six mini screens alongside the files displayed ever changing sections of the emporium and she could see Mimi on a screen with a couple of customers. She was more than happy to wait for her opting to settle in the cosy scroll back, armchair next to the desk. She was fascinated by the changing screens on the monitors as the shop seemed to be laid out with in different styles stretching across various periods of history. One of the screens displayed a Victorian sitting room and alongside it was a dining room clearly from the 1970's. It was a great idea and Lottie mused on how interesting it must be when new stock arrived. How did they choose which room or was it always obvious?

The voices started to become louder as the troop moved back towards the reception area. Mimi was suddenly in front of her with the two clients confirming they would ring her later in the day once they knew if the dimensions worked in their room. She gave them her business card and moved from the clients to embrace Lottie warmly exclaiming "*Ma chère, bienvenue!*" Lottie hugged her warmly and accepted the three kisses on her cheeks whilst rather clumsily air-kissing her in return.

Whilst waiting for Mimi to lock up at lunchtime, Lottie asked if she could have a look around the *brocante* as the concept of individual rooms was surprisingly attractive. The building seemed to stretch back much further than she had first imagined as she passed through the various mini rooms until she was near the far wall. There was a door leading through to what looked like a workshop come storeroom and she assumed this was where the deliveries arrived before items were sorted into the respective rooms. She could understand how easy it would be to buy something from the emporium as prices started low on the accessories and increased upwards for the more expensive, collectable furniture. A system of coloured dots was painted discretely on the items and Lottie made a note to check with Mimi what they all meant as some were red whilst others were yellow and green.

As they drove to one of Mimi's favourite restaurants in St-Rémy-de-Provence, they both chatted about Lottie's Bed and Breakfast location and what she had been doing since she arrived. They could enjoy a leisurely meal as one of the other traders was working at the *brocante* in the afternoon and Mimi's only time constraint was a meeting with her solicitor at half past six. She explained that she

table, declined an aperitif and decided to send WhatsApp messages to the kids. She was just finishing off when Mimi arrived appearing a little flustered at being late and bemoaning the appalling lack of street parking in Avignon where every meter seemed to be on a short time limit or permits were required. She slumped down in her chair and ordered two glasses of champagne leaving Lottie laughing and uttering "*ooh la la!*" in her best French accent.

Apparently, the solicitor's meeting had gone satisfactorily and Mimi was now at liberty to sell the *brocante* and her stock in addition to releasing her contract on the apartment. Lottie recalled the coloured dots on many items in the shop and asked her what they meant as Mimi explained that two other people used her building to sell their items. It was not uncommon in France and every item was listed on the *brocante's* computer noting who owned what merchandise, the maximum amount of discount that could be offered, and a note of where the item had been sourced with the purchase date. Mimi charged her two aides a monthly rent which they were happy to continue to receive whilst the business was sold. Lottie explained that she worked in an antique shop two afternoons a week and recounted her days as a theatre Prop Master. She spoke of the regular calls from the Parisian antique shop, "*Le Corbeau*", when they were seeking quintessential British furniture giving Mimi reason to declare that for every French Napoleonic bed there was a Thomas Chippendale chair requested by someone else. The region was extremely popular for holiday-home owners and Mimi described an international client base who sought to furnish their second homes with the *brocante's* items.

It was with a huge sadness that Lottie hugged Mimi as the evening came to a close. She had been such a genuine and kind friend and Lottie walked back to the *chambre d'hôte* feeling quite despondent at leaving this jewel of a city. The next morning, Lottie had arranged a taxi to the airport as she didn't want to risk searching for buses or missing the flight. She looked over at the Palais des Papes and promised she would return some day as she'd hardly touched the surface of exploring Avignon.

CHAPTER THREE
MUM, ARE YOU MAD?

Lottie's dream of how she'd arrived in Avignon suddenly jolted her awake and she lay in bed for a while partly exhausted by it and partly listening to the quiet hum of Avignon's traffic; those poor sleepy heads setting out so early for their place of work. She turned over, cuddled the pillow to her stomach and returned to a foetal position. She allowed her thoughts to drift back to Avignon, Mimi and her eventual decision that would bring her back to the city. She gave in to the final part of her transition from the UK as her dream absorbed the noise of the plane's engines heralding her return to UK soil.

Lottie's flight landed on time and Lou met her at the airport. She wasn't sure why she felt so disenchanted to be home or why she was lacking any enthusiasm for her Buckinghamshire life. She was genuinely happy to see her daughter, exchange their news and to know she could easily ring Ali and Tom tonight. She caught up on emails and post including signing papers to transfer Bob's business to Ed and Clive. She loaded the washing machine and smiled at the odour on the blouse she'd worn in the café that first night. Fortunately, none of the family smoked and so the memories flooded back as she sniffed the cigarette fumes clinging to her clothes. Smoking still seemed really popular in the South although she'd seen quite a few people vaping with e-cigarettes.

She popped to the supermarket to grab something for the next few days and treated herself to a Côte de Rhône red wine to relive the memories which were fading only too rapidly.

She spent an uneventful week helping out at the two shops admitting to herself that she felt distracted and unfulfilled for the first time since she'd begun working there. She went to the gym with Jules and went to a photography exhibition with Jill but nothing seemed to lift a malaise that she was in a rut and she questioned whether this was to be her life at fifty-six. She needed a project but something was telling her that she needed much, much more than that. She wanted a challenge that would throw her life up in the air, shake her firmly and turn everything she knew on its head. A fresh start, a new chapter ...... no, a new book was required! She'd had the germ of an idea on the plane back to the UK which seemed to pop into her head at all times of the day. The worst time was at night when she lay in bed trying to fall asleep but it would also earworm its way back in as she gradually woke up in the morning. Those typical moments when thoughts that you'd pushed away during the day suddenly came back insisting to be recognised, dissected and a decision taken.

She realised that Marlow offered a comfortable life but she couldn't picture her future now that Bob was gone and the children were all independent. She was already frustrated after one week helping at the shops. Could she envisage meeting someone new? She found that concept very difficult indeed and felt exhausted by the thought of starting again. She decided to ring Alex about her idea and seek his counsel. He confirmed he would need to check her figures again; large numbers in a bank account which were destined to stay there if she carried on with no adjustment to her life. She would need to talk to Mimi but she found herself thinking "I could try". Then she exclaimed out loud and to no one in particular "Yes, I could try! What's the worst that could happen? Just sodding do it you wimp."

Alex was understandably cautious about his sister's significant change of lifestyle but Lottie recognised that he was never particularly impulsive nor a risk taker. He pointed out some of the downsides, the obvious and the not so obvious and Lottie confirmed she would consider all of his points and his sage advice. The next day she rang Mimi who was delighted to hear from her but was clearly very surprised at her proposal. She advised she'd email the accounts within the next couple of days which proved to be dormant hours which Lottie spent stressing about her intended future career. On receipt of the figures, which included a generous offer to transfer the rental of Mimi's apartment into her name, she forwarded everything to her brother, Alex, for his consideration. She sat back to await his feedback which came back within a couple of hours causing her to ring Mimi and place a verbal offer on her business and flat.

Lottie was about to buy the *brocante* and all the stock that was owned by Mireille Rivaud. She'd kept the same arrangement with the two other vendors renting the space and she now had responsibility for a handyman come furniture shifter. She was fully committed to running the antique emporium in the South of France and she grinned like a Cheshire cat and felt like celebrating. Lottie chuckled as she remembered the flustered Mimi sinking into the restaurant chair and demanding two flutes of champagne. They'd be very welcome right now!

Lottie didn't fully discount the family's advice or the challenging arguments against her decision. A warning light flashed in her head that she might need a "Plan B" if she was not successful at her new business venture. She decided to contact rental agencies in the morning as she realised that, should she want to return to the UK, then she really did not want to start house hunting again. Anyway, the market had moved so much since she'd bought the house with Bob that she would never find anything again within the price range and with the same comforts. The rental idea helped her sleep soundly as she fell into bed exhausted by the continual rush of adrenalin at the thought of the coming months

Speaking to Mimi in the evening, she agreed to check for flights and would rebook the room with Inès. Her brand-new friend agreed to set up an appointment with her solicitor, known as a *notaire,* which was obligatory for the business transfer and he could also redraw the contracts with the other vendors using the *brocante.* They'd been in place for years and it was time to make a marginal increase and the change in ownership provided the right catalyst. *"N'inquiètes Lottie, les deux seront contents"* Mimi reassured feeling certain they would both be happy with a modest increase given the utility costs and the taxes had all increased over the years. Alain, the furniture mover and all-round handyman, only worked twenty hours a week and was paid by a system run by *CESU,* a self-employed system managed by the government, which Mimi would explain when she came over. Lottie was already thinking about future plans for the *brocante* and spent the rest of the call talking to Mimi about renting out items as television or theatre props. Mimi had never considered this but the businesswomen in her recognised the potential for items making money via rental if they were not sold. Lottie returned to her days as Henley Theatre's prop master advising Mimi that she often used prop houses to hire items on long term rental for the wide variety of plays, sometimes modern furnishings and sometimes period productions. Whilst at these prop house premises, there were no end of television designers and prop buyers, also seeking out a list of furniture and dressing props for their studio and film locations. There was no issue that Lottie could foresee in making it a rental facility unless Mimi thought the business rules within France would scotch her plans. Mimi confirmed that it was a great idea and she'd ring ahead to the notaire to explain the additional function which would need to be added to the business registration.

Lottie's thoughts returned to renting out her home. Ali was happy to manage Bob's apartments but she wasn't convinced she'd have the time to manage the house as well. She decided she should place it with a Marlow company and checked the going monthly rate for a three-bedroomed house with garden and called one of the many estate agencies to arrange an appointment.

What an incredible week! When she'd looked across at the Palais des Papes on that last morning, she'd had no idea that her return to the city would be so rapid. For the first time in a couple of months, she felt elated, decisive and, most definitely, contented. The phone lines and the Skype calls were in a constant "busy" state as Mimi and Lottie exchanged questions and answers over the coming weeks. Everything was shaping up and the list of outstanding tasks was diminishing in line with the number of days before Lottie's departure. She'd decided to rent a transit van to move her clothes, shoes, and various items from the house that the renters would not need or expect to find at the property. She'd been incredibly lucky as the agency had found an American couple in their early 60s who needed to be close to Henley Business School. Walt and Elizabeth Cadougan would be on a three-year secondment from the USA with him lecturing in Executive Education as part of the school's MBA diploma. The couple already knew the Marlow area quite well and loved the town and its riverside setting. They didn't particularly want to be in Henley or in close proximity to Walt's day job.

Lou and Martin had already offered to drive the transit on the planned weekend of departure allowing Martin to be at the nursery during the week and only Lou to arrange Saturday cover for the shop. Lottie was relieved even though she would have been happy to drive across France on her own. The company would be reassuring on such a long journey and she'd need someone to share the kilometres if they were to reach Avignon within the same day. She would also need to return the transit van as it would have cost a small fortune to have left it at a partner location in Avignon.

The weeks soon flew by and Lottie's only regret was not meeting the couple about to rent the house. Unfortunately, the dates didn't align meaning she would need to leave the agency to show them the house but at least she'd prepared a comprehensive list of notes for them. It had been an interrupted sleep of constantly checking the clock when a grey sky of the breaking dawn announced the early hour of departure from the UK. Lottie didn't really know how she felt as they left England and her family and friends. She was excited for the adventure that lay ahead but she felt guilty at leaving the children and sad to leave her friends. There'd been a couple of evenings at local restaurants to toast her new project and Barbara had given her three beautiful books on antiques and a really useful guide to furniture and accessories throughout the decades. The latter would be an incredible reference book for her idea to hire out items to TV and theatre companies. Tom had come up from Cornwall although Isabella was not with him as she was four weeks away from "popping" and they both felt it was too risky.

The weary travellers arrived in Avignon at quarter past seven in the evening. They'd done well and only stopped for a toilet break, coffee and some sandwiches. Mimi was already at the apartment when they arrived which allowed Lou and Martin to meet her for the first time and maybe the only time. The apartment was spacious with high ceilings and large bay windows. As expected, the furnishings were tasteful and the larger wooden items beautifully in-keeping with the chic façade and the interior of the building.

Fortunately, Lottie's monthly rental to Walt and Elizabeth Cadougan more than met the monthly rental on Mimi's apartment. She might need the difference between the two rental amounts as she had no idea how much utilities might cost in France plus there were two tax bills called *Taxe d'habitation* and *Taxes Foncières* which would need to be paid at the end of the year. These outgoings would affect her living expenses in Avignon and there was yet another set for the business. Lottie had done her sums several times and felt comfortable that she was well within her limits as long as she didn't wait too long for the shop to provide a monthly income.

They offloaded Lottie's effects and their host rustled up a pasta dish followed by a divine caramel and chocolate dessert and an excellent bottle of Tavel wine. They traded stories all evening about the two families and Fleur rang after dinner to wish Lottie every success with the business venture and her life in Avignon. By midnight, everyone's eyes were drooping. Lou and Martin shared a rustic, painted settee bed in the sitting room and Lottie had the spare room.

Mimi was scheduled to leave Tuesday morning after they'd both been to the meeting with her solicitor and been to the Tax Office on Monday. She'd already taken a number of items up to Paris as Fleur had found her a lovely roof top apartment in the 19th district, or arrondissement as they called it. She was very excited about the apartment and not least because it was only four metro stops from her daughter who lived in Montmartre. Fleur lived in an adorable house just off the large square which was home to the Sacré Coeur and to the many painters and caricaturists. She'd acquired it from Madame de Parade who had spotted Fleur's potential from Day One at the House of Dior and had become her mentor. Madame de Parade had no children to inherit her house and, therefore, it came as no surprise to the employees that the house was bequeathed to Fleur on her death. It was a little gold mine in one of Paris' much sought-after romantic districts and Fleur thanked Madame de Parade every day she put her key in the door and stepped into the irrestibly unique property.

Her mother would soon be nearby in the trendy 19th district of Butte-Chaumont. The apartment was near the Canal Saint-Denis and Fleur had found it for her having viewed more than ten before inviting Mimi to grab a train ticket "tout de suite" if she was to like it and wanted to sign a contract. Like any capital anywhere in the world, these apartments never stayed available longer than a few hours and salaries were inflated, if necessary, to acquire the right building in the right district. Happily, Madame Rivaud represented a more mature lady and was not going to be partying until the early of the morning with transitory types in and out of her home, so she passed the necessary hurdles and gained occupancy with little fuss. She suspected the keen eye of the all-knowing concierge might have been involved in the decision.

This was to be a new chapter for her too and she felt a genuine sense of relief that she could see her daughter more readily than the odd occasion when work allowed her to take a holiday. She was no stranger to Paris and its districts and looked forward to exploring them again without the need to visit the flea markets known as *puces* for little jewels to take back to the *brocante* in Avignon. Her roof terrace gave her all the exterior space that she needed and she had the parks on her doorstep should she feel the need to visit wide open spaces. She particularly liked the suspended walkway in Parc des Buttes Chaumont as the "*passerelle supendue*" allowed such a verdant view of the park and the neighbouring buildings.

On Sunday, Mimi and Lottie went to the *brocante* as Mimi wanted to explain the files and paperwork. Lottie had already created a new trading name which would be "*Les Trésors de Ma Famille*" as Mimi had said the press announcements would need to be prepared and ready for printing after the solicitor's meeting. They walked into the courtyard where the flowers had been replaced by the season's new arrivals. Lottie reflected on her first visit and how far she had physically and mentally progressed since walking into this antiquarian empire to meet Mimi in person some months ago. She marvelled at how quickly the friendship had developed and inwardly laughed once more at what Bob would make of her future plans.

They spent almost the whole day going through the files with Mimi explaining the process for incoming and outgoing stock. She also gave Lottie a good insight into the characters of the two other vendors outlining the strengths and weaknesses of Francine Besnier and Claude Tourand. She spoke about Alain who was responsible for moving the larger items from the workshop or delivery point to their new location in the selected room of choice and then moving sold items back again for collection or delivery. He was a versatile chap and could turn his hand to small electrical and plumbing repairs and was a real godsend. Mimi explained how the *CESU* system worked and how he got paid. Lastly, she listed the various young artisans and their responsibilities as all of them were an integral part of the *brocante*'s success. These were the artisans who restored, repainted, rebuilt, rewired, re-glued, and made new stock presentable and saleable. They each had their own talents and could be contacted on an ad hoc basis and were willing to work per quote, per item. Each one was detailed by Mimi outlining their expertise and who worked easily without her pressing for completion and others that would rather work a morning and drink away the afternoon and evening. She said the latter presented a problem,but the extraordinary calibre of their work meant she tolerated the need to stay on top of their individual projects.

Lottie's notebook bulged with all of the information and she couldn't wait to transfer it onto her laptop and put it all into some semblance of order. Mimi tended to hop from one subject to the next and then back with a small bite of information about the previous subject, so Lottie had arrows plastered up and down against the headings. Lottie was not short of questions on every part of the handover. She had pages of questions which she'd created back in the UK as she thought about the transfer of knowledge and advice.

It was a juggling act trying to feed these in at a relevant point in the exchange.

By late afternoon they had come to a full stop. Mimi said that it was now a case of Lottie taking the reins and ringing her if anything new came to pass that have not been covered in the handover. She'd admired the copious notes that Lottie had taken and didn't doubt that her past experience and her attention to detail would create a thriving business. All that remained was for her to donate a parting gift causing Lottie to look at her quizzically and question the reason for a present. Mimi went back into the workshop and came back with a very large box that she placed on the Louis XVII desk in the office area.

Lottie removed the bright red bow and a card in Mimi's handwriting containing a touching message. She lifted the lid and inside the box was the wrought iron sign that had been beautifully repainted and announced *"Les Trésors de Ma Famille"*. Lottie gasped at the touching gesture and felt hugely emotional to receive such a thoughtful and personal gift from Mimi. It must be an emotional wrench as she, too, turned to a fresh chapter in the new book that was to be her life from Tuesday morning.

"Les Antiquités de Mimi" had been painted over and the new silver sign containing the name of the new business sat within the outline of a shield. The inside of the shield was painted blue with Mimi pointing to it and declaring *"La Manche"*; the English Channel that had been between them. The conjoined hands below the name of the shop represented their friendship but could also be Lottie's gesture to future clients. It was an impeccable alteration which perfectly captured their friendship. *"Laissez dans la boîte, ma chère, Lucas s'occupera demain"* Mimi instructed

her friend who rightly assumed Lucas was the metalwork artisan who would come and rehang the sign tomorrow. Lottie kissed and hugged her enthusiastically and proffered her clean hankie as they both sniffed and wiped away the unexpected tears.

If Sunday had been busy then Monday was a full-blown whirlwind of meetings with the solicitor, the tax office and the office controlling the business registration. Her file of papers bulged under the weight of the additional documents that each service handed to her as proof of her new business. The business registration number would follow within the next few weeks, however, she could start trading immediately. By the end of the day, she was totally exhausted and her head was spinning from an exhaustive list of business French vocabulary. At various stages in the day she'd found herself leaning heavily on Mimi for translations to all manner of legalese which sounded very confusing. She would never have coped on her own but then she would never have set out to buy the *brocante* without her friend's appreciable assistance. Lottie would have loved to have gone back to the apartment and had a quiet dinner with Mimi, however, other plans were afoot. A dinner had been arranged at a restaurant in Avignon with Claude and Francine. It was the last piece in the jigsaw before Mimi felt she could depart and leave Lottie in charge of her business. When Mimi and Lottie returned to the apartment, Mimi poured them both a flute of champagne to celebrate their day. Lottie braced herself not to fall asleep with a combination of alcohol and extreme tiredness. After two flutes of champagne, she declared she needed a cold shower to wake herself up and enliven her sagging body. She dressed in the closest item she had that looked French which was a dress that still fell over her knees. In her mind she looked decidedly "British". Mimi laughed at her cries of angst whilst looking her usual fabulous self in a tiny leather jacket, chinos, a frilly, cream blouse and velvet slip-on shoes.

They had a lovely dinner which immediately assuaged Mimi's concerns as her two friends and Lottie bonded within minutes of meeting each other. Claude was very entertaining recounting stories of a lost youth in Gloucester when he was staying with his UK pen pal and Francine could not have been sweeter repeatedly reminding Lottie that she could call her at any time if she had questions. Mimi was scheduled to get the 10h45 train from the TGV station just outside Avignon and Lottie would drive her there in her newly acquired Renault Estate. It was Mimi's car of choice even with 70,000 kilometres on the clock as the hatchback had been extremely useful transporting small furniture items to buyers or picking up small consignments from sellers. She would have no need for a car in Paris as she'd go everywhere by metro, taxi or bus and, in any case, there was nowhere to park. In contrast, Lottie would definitely need a left-hand drive vehicle, so the transfer made perfect sense. It had turned midnight when they fell into their respective beds with Mimi feeling "job done" and Lottie feeling like she'd done twelve rounds with Muhammed Ali.

Lottie chose to remain closed for one week to bring herself up to speed on the stock and understand who owned what items. She was like a little kid in a candy shop when she walked into the *brocante* and turned the key in the lock on her first trading day. She headed to the kitchen to make a coffee humming one her favourite jazz songs in Bob's collection. Her mobile started to ping as good luck messages came in from children and friends wishing her well and lots of success. She loved this giant prop house that was fifty times larger than the storeroom back at Henley Theatre. She had shoved a few of her reference books into her bag for the quiet moments between browsers and buyers. Lottie congratulated herself on using her evenings before leaving the UK for a crash course in French and also to read the reference books to familiarise herself again with antiques. She felt comfortable recognising the giveaway signs of a change of leg in furniture or a style of silverware and glass that would help indicate the century or the decade. She had never felt more prepared or knowledgeable since before giving birth to Lou.

Many of the tools that Mimi used to attract stock such as advertising in local and regional newspapers or offering house clearance facilities were continued by Lottie. She notified the various companies of the change of contact details. She was loving every minute of her new life and spent every long weekend exploring the region as and when Francine and Claude were at the helm. It wasn't until a photo of Tom and Isabella's new baby appeared on "WhatsApp" that she suddenly felt every kilometre of distance between them and her life in France. She couldn't just down tools and go and visit them, hold Regina Roberta Pearce for herself or care for Isabella and Thomas during the huge transition in the couple's life. No, this was the definite downside of living in another country. Even just being "next door" in France did not make the move any easier to reconcile in Lottie's head. She knew from the start that it would be a negative when events and problems affected her children but she had offset the need for her own development as all her children had partners to lean on and she was the one with no emotional support. She replied insisting on a load more photos and promised to Skype them both that evening. There was a baby shop just off Rue Vernet so she'd head there to buy them something on Thursday.

She'd already done a couple of house clearance jobs when she had her third one scheduled in the diary for the following week. It did not go as well as the others for a number of reasons; mainly the death of Jean-Louis Pislait which had resulted in her meeting Brigadier-Chef Lepireon of the *Police Municipale*. Cédric Mallet lived in Avignon and was moving to a retirement home on the other side of the river in Villeneuve-les-Avignon. The responsibility of his home and its extensive garden had become too much for him; particularly given his last fall in which he broke his hip. The accident was just another reason added to a long list telling him he had to relinquish his independence.

Lottie was greeted by an eighty-year-old man of slight build and tiny in stature. He cut a chipper figure in his immaculate dress of grey blazer and black trousers and there was a twinkle in his eye that was clearly for the ladies in his life. Within a smattering of sentences, it was clear to Lottie that he was not looking forward to the retirement home as he enjoyed a level of independence that he would lose within the coming months. Monsieur Mallet had drawn up a list of items, taken the measurements and even proffered an indication of price. He was extremely organised and very much in charge of the deportation of his life's possessions.

It didn't surprise Lottie that he had enjoyed an interesting career before his retirement. Lottie's English accent would always be very evident to any French person and, as they walked from room to room, he explained that he'd worked for Renault for many years including five years in London. He'd been responsible for promoting their new product releases across several of the city's garages. He'd also been one of the many drivers in Renault's Racing Team, so he was no stranger to many of the racing circuits in Great Britain. His English accent was impeccable even though he'd not had reason to use the language for many, many years. He said he listened to audio books in French but he missed the dry humour of the British, so he'd also purchased English audio stories in order to maintain his accent and grow his vocabulary.

Whilst Cédric Mallet had been with the Racing Team, he had suffered a life-changing accident and had subsequently had to leave Renault and retrain. As it fitted with his hobby, he'd opted to work with leather goods and trained how to tool leather and to create intricate and complex designs on a variety of items. It had been a profitable business for him and his wife for the remaining business years as there were few people skilled in this very individual artistry. Perhaps in an effort to keep Lottie a bit longer, he invited her to a glass of wine and proceeded to dig out photos of the leather merchandise that his wife had photographed prior to him selling them. There was no doubting his skill which had also been noted by a fashion house who had employed him periodically to create pricey and exclusive pieces such as hip flasks and business card holders. Lottie questioned whether he missed the work and Cédric confirmed those days were now long gone as his arthritic hands could no longer angle the tools in the manner required. He still had an opportunity to appreciate and recognise excellent artistry, therefore, he was delighted to use this knowledge to help his nephew, Jean-Louis, in a small project relating to tooled leather books. She could understand his desire to feel needed and have a sense of purpose in life no matter what age and asked him to explain about the project.

Cédric announced that he'd just received four books and he would show them to Lottie who was bewitched by the examples in front of her. Each one was strikingly different in design, colour and feel. The book in her hand had a ruby red tooled leather cover with a black liner under the red hide. Intricate cuts and holes had been made to the leather to create a design that was mystical, magical and the work looked like a bedazzling jewel. Inside was an ecclesiastical book with large, illuminated letters and tiny images heralding the start of each new chapter in the individual tome. Lottie was in awe of the cover and its contents. The next book had a yellow liner under a deep midnight blue cover that contained a creation of small stars and a cream-coloured moon. Yet again, she was transported and this time to a scene from the folklore tales of the Arabian Nights. Lottie placed the two books on a side table to study the remaining two. The third book was housed in a brown leather cover with an orange and gold liner. It was as if she'd been dropped in the Sahara Desert as she stared at the detail of the complex tooling. The fourth book was green and brown and she imagined walking across a forest floor with the damp air hanging low in the trees and animals and insects scurrying from her feet. All of the interiors appeared to contain copies of ancient sacred texts.

Cédric confirmed that his nephew had arranged for them to be sent to him and his role was to provide an estimated cost based on each book's detail and skill. He usually received a delivery per month and really enjoyed reviewing the designs by the different artisans. The small job kept him in touch with changing fashions and he always earned a few euros from his nephew. Lottie acknowledged the beauty and skill of each of the books and surprisingly found herself asking if she could buy them causing Cédric to question whether she had a buyer. Lottie confirmed that she did not but that she loved the works of art so much that she could already see them sitting in the various rooms at the *brocante*. The elderly man confirmed that he had already costed the books and his nephew would only be selling them anyway so he could not see a problem. Lottie was elated and wrote out a cheque so she could take them with her. Before leaving she had to sit through a number of Cédric's photo albums as he showed her some faded photos of his early days in London, then a few of his sister and his nephew and it was a further half hour before she could escape confirming she'd ring him in the morning with a price for the furniture. She walked to the car with her precious items congratulating herself on abstaining from the second glass of wine.

She had agreed to be at the shop the following morning even though it was Friday and Francine's shift. She had her first meeting with a small, independent television company who were coming to hire items for a drama production. She hadn't had time to explain the paperwork to her or to Claude, so it made sense to receive the designer and his assistant herself. The set designer provided a précis of the storyline and characters so that Lottie could offer suggestions for the furniture and accessories. The gang of three spent nearly three hours selecting the various items. When the assistant mentioned the main character was well travelled, Lottie thought of the tooled leather books and wondered if they might be of interest. She was delighted that her idea was not only acknowledged but that the four books were added to the props list without further comment. Lottie double- checked the list of items with the prop buyer and advised they would be moved to the delivery point by the following afternoon. She confirmed that the physical loading would be the responsibility of the company, the despatch paperwork would accompany the items and the order would be sent electronically within forty-eight hours. She poured them both a coffee and chatted with them on a personal and professional level in anticipation of future business or "word of mouth" advertising back at their office. It had been a successful visit and another "first" on Lottie's project list.

CHAPTER FOUR
THE BUBBLE BURSTS

Lottie drove into the courtyard Wednesday morning all set for a quiet day. Alain needed to find a new home for some of the stock in the delivery area that Claude had delivered yesterday evening. She had just got the coffee machine prepared when the phone rang in the office and she traipsed back hoping her caffeine fix would not be delayed too long.

She started with her usual welcome but was cut off abruptly as a male voice demanded the return of his uncle's books in an aggressive and difficult to understand French patois. Lottie was perplexed and couldn't immediately grasp what he said as she weighed up the man's atypical introduction. Given her lack of response, he insisted again and with a little more information. "Madame, you came to my uncle's house and purchased his items including four leather-backed books. I need the books returned and will pay the same price". Lottie could feel the hairs on the back of her neck bristle. This guy was not only rude but she couldn't understand how Cédric Mallet, who had such a gentle manner, could tolerate this oaf even if he was his nephew. She found herself explaining in French "even if I could return them, then I can't" which, on reflection, didn't make sense to her in English let alone in French. The nephew shouted "*quoi?*" down the phone line and Lottie found herself explaining that the books were on hire to a theatre company". She was so rattled that she made a mistake given it was a television company but by then she'd realised she'd stick with the error as something about the man's phone manner was extremely unsettling. The nephew insisted she contact the company and get them returned by the weekend as he would come to the premises himself to collect them; his name was Jean-Louis Pislait. Lottie confirmed that it was unlikely she would be successful and privately resolved not to contact them. He reiterated his demand and that he would be at the *brocante* on Saturday. She took his contact details and noted his name. "Pissy by name, pissy by nature" she thought to herself having no idea that the man would end his days under the wheels of a truck in Rue de la République.

She hung up and went to get her cup of coffee. The call had really unsettled her and she chastised herself for buying the books even though they'd been so striking and were possibly quite rare. She decided not to contact Cédric as he wasn't to blame for his very rude nephew and why should he be criticised for selling the books? She preferred to ring Claude to forewarn him of the man's arrival on Saturday and explained that the books were out on loan to a television company and she had no intention of contacting them. Claude confirmed that it would be bad practice, particularly given it was the first rental, so told her not to worry but he appreciated the "heads up" on the visit.

She was exploring the pretty, hilltop village of Ménerbes when she heard her mobile ringing in her bag. It was no surprise that it was Claude as she'd expected his call during the day. Monsieur Pislait was in front of him and refusing to leave without confirmation of the name of the company using "his" books. Lottie requested to speak to him and fudged replying directly when Pislait was shouting down the phone. She said that the company could not release them as they were integral to the story. According to Claude, he handed the phone back to him and stormed out muttering "*ce n'est pas finis*". Claude's own portrayal of Cédric's relative left her hoping that he would not return. She popped into a café that had a terrace overlooking the fields of vines across to the neighbouring hills. The village of Ménerbes was a wonderful mix of stone houses and small lanes. It was also one of those villages that was hard work on the knees and difficult to imagine carrying a load of shopping up to a house with no road access or one without a garage. She bought herself a soft drink and sat out on the terrace overlooking the vines to let the view erase the words of the odious Monsieur Pislait.

Lottie had a busy Sunday ringing the family and catching up on news of Regina who was now beginning to focus on faces and hand movements. She also contacted Mimi who was loving every minute of her Parisian lifestyle. They swopped notes on what they loved and what they disliked. Her friend was missing walking into the garden and picking her own fruit and Lottie was struggling with France's inability to say "sorry" when someone messed up. Lottie updated Mimi on the events at the shop including her first rental to a television company. She briefly mentioned Cédric Mallet's skilfully crafted books and the ensuing problem but far preferred to hear of Mimi's news and the various restaurants that she'd discovered with Fleur. She hoped she might be able to accept an invitation to visit in a few weeks if the workload permitted. That had them both laughing as Mimi acknowledged Lottie's workload and congratulated her on the various sales and the rental. She was delighted and proud of her friend's early rental success and the potential value of this additional enterprise.

Lottie was surprised at how composed she was on entering the *brocante* on Monday when she found the lock had been forced. Her dealings so far with Jean-Louis Pislait and his words that "the matter was not finished" left her assuming that he might up the ante even though she could not automatically assume his involvement. She switched on the lights and nervously looked at the cameras which were still showing the various furnished room and her eyes took in the filing cabinets that were pulled open and the files scattered across the desk. There was no doubt in her mind who had been the intruder however, as there was no camera in the office, she doubted there would be any proof.

She played back the tapes of the rooms which endorsed no one had passed beyond the office and therefore nothing was stolen. She rang the police who advised her to come down to the station and they would provide a crime reference number or "*une plainte*" for her insurer. As there was a hefty excess on the policy, Lottie decided to pay a locksmith to fix the door rather than make a claim although she still obtained the reference number when she called into the station later in the day. The locksmith turned up late morning, looked over the mechanism and doorframe, uttered the equivalent of "see you later" and disappeared off until three o'clock. He returned with a 5-way lock that fitted across five points of the door and would prevent any further problems. She rang Claude to update him and he naturally asked if the paperwork for the television company had been stolen. Lottie advised that it was still in her briefcase as she'd wanted to transfer the data onto her laptop and onto a separate financial sheet that she was maintaining for rentals. Jean-Louis Pislait had broken in but he had learned no more than he knew before ... well less as he was still under the illusion it was a theatre company and neither she nor Claude had corrected him.

Whilst the locksmith fitted the new mechanism, Philippe one of the cabinet restorers popped in to return a restored ebony table with a mother-of-pearl inlay. He came up to see Lottie who was keeping a watchful eye on the work to the door. He'd done a beautiful marquetry job restoring a damaged side table and Lottie arranged his payment whilst he went to make a *noisette* coffee. He listened to all that had happened whilst smoking two cigarettes and getting a coffee refill. He was wired with adrenalin from all the stimulants as he tutted and expressed the occasional "*putain*" throughout Lottie recounting the events. The locksmith also joined in the conversation uttering "*La France est pleine de connards, Madame, n'est ce pas?*" Lottie made a mental note to check what a *connard* was so she neither confirmed nor denied his statement. Philippe suggested buying an additional camera for the office area which he thought Alain could fit to the existing system or maybe it could run independently. It was a helpful observation that would have been useful in the past seventy-two hours.

Lottie was touched as he then steered the conversation to ask after her and that he hoped she was not too shaken. He greatly admired this British lady, recently widowed and beginning a new life in a foreign country. He could not imagine any of the women in his family making such a decision. She confirmed that she was fine and that the biggest annoyance was the cost of repairing the door even though she'd yet to see the invoice which would make her wonder where the locksmith had parked his Ferrari. Philippe insisted she ring him at any time of the day or night if she was in trouble and needed help. He urged her to key his number into her mobile phone and, when she waivered, he picked it up and shoved it into her hand reading out his number so she couldn't object. He would be honoured to help her no matter how trivial a problem and no matter what time of day. Lottie had not witnessed anyone worrying about her for months and felt touched by Philippe's words which made her feel emotional and just a little teary. It was a huge relief when the phone rang and put paid to Lottie's quivering lip.

After Philippe and the locksmith had left, she decided to ring Monsieur Mallet. She wanted to learn a little more about his nephew and how much of a threat he might be. Cédric answered the phone and listened to Madame Pearce's explanation of the phone call and his nephew's threatening visit on the Saturday. He seemed genuinely surprised and very distressed as Lottie added news of the break-in that had occurred somewhere between Saturday evening and this morning. The line went quiet and she wondered if she'd overstepped the mark and he was unwell. Lottie confirmed that she did not want him to mention her call and that she only needed to know a bit more about why his nephew was so anxious to have the books back in his possession. Cédric Mallet couldn't identify any reason but confirmed Jean-Louis had been furious with him for selling them. All he knew was Jean-Louis had experienced a difficult childhood which was to cause him problems later in life and he was only too glad that his life seemed to be back on an even keel after a period in prison. He reaffirmed the books arrived every month, he costed them, and he believed they were sold to churches, cathedrals, galleries and private collectors. He didn't know the mark-up on his price or whether the business was profitable. By chance, and some months ago, one of the deliveries had arrived with an invoice and he knew the books were still pricy irrespective of Cédric's own assessment which usually increased their individual cost. He reiterated that he was sorry Madame Pearce had been upset and that he would not mention her call to his nephew. He would be moving to the residential home next week and he knew the deliveries were scheduled to be sent to him at Villeneuve-les-Avignon. This delighted him as he really enjoyed the opportunity to see the skills of each of the different artisans which varied from delivery to delivery. Lottie thanked him, told him not to worry as it was probably just the shock that one of the deliveries had been sold direct and his nephew had not been in charge of the sale. Cédric rather weakly acknowledged that she might be correct.

Daily routines continued for Francine, Claude and Lottie over the next few days. Alain had located a tiny camera that would fit easily onto one of the office's wall lights and it recorded to her laptop via the internet. It was inexpensive and gave the team some additional security even though the system was reliant upon the internet which was not infallible.

Lottie woke as her alarm clock sprang into action filling the bedroom with a Claude Francois 1970's hit called "Alexandrie Alexandra". She punched "snooze" as she wasn't ready for such an up tempo start to her day; *France Bleu's* radio station abruptly disappeared. Lottie's meander from leaving the UK to the pursuit by Jean-Louis Pislait and his subsequent death had ended. Her head throbbed and a light sweat had formed across her temple. In her dream, momentarily a nightmare, she had imagined him catching up with her and flashing a knife across her throat in a threatening manner. She realised it was ridiculous as the man had died but she couldn't shirk the fact that the monk was still out there and he appeared to have been focused on her and Pislait.

She reluctantly jumped out of bed, headed to the kitchen to make a coffee and thought about the day ahead. She decided to go and visit Cédric Mallet as he'd mentioned the name of the retirement home. It wasn't difficult to find it in France's equivalent of the Yellow Pages which were similarly known as "*Pages Jaunes*". Lottie felt somehow involved in his nephew's death even though it was a ridiculous thought given she'd every right to purchase the books. She signed in at Reception and headed down the corridor to his room. Tapping lightly on the door, she put her ear to the wooden panel to listen out for signs of movement within. She heard him groan as he lifted himself out of a chair and the door opened to present the whippet-like elderly man with the twinkly eyes. Lottie asked if she could come in and he opened the door with a broad smile exclaiming how delighted he was to see her again. "*Je peux vous offrir quelque chose, Madame Pearce?*" he enquired as he pointed to his little larder of items next to a tray of china cups. She readily accepted a mint tea as they exchanged pleasantries whilst he prepared the drinks.

Once he had sunk back into his armchair and Lottie was sitting uncomfortably on one of his upright chairs that she recognised from the house, she began her message of condolence for his nephew. She lied saying that she'd read of his demise in the local paper so as to avoid any complicated questions. Cédric was not as upset as she imagined he would be and, surprisingly, there were no tears or need to console him as she had expected. She sat quietly as he explained the background to his sister's only son; the complicated upbringing before his tranquil life in *L'Abbaye de Notre Croix de Fer*. At the mention of an abbey, the image of the monk following Jean-Louis came rushing into Lottie's head. She tried not to imagine what the connection might be or the nature of their relationship preferring instead to concentrate on Cédric's story. She still didn't want to admit to being present on the day of his death so referenced his nephew's visit to see Claude on Saturday when he'd apparently turned up in a brown suit and not a monk's habit. Cédric confirmed that he didn't wear a robe all the time as it rather depended on what he was doing and who he was meeting.

His nephew's childhood had been very difficult as his mother had married a man who was no stranger to beating his wife as and when the mood took him and particularly when he'd sunk too many glasses of pastis. Jean-Louis had often defended his mother over the years and suffered many a brutal pummelling. Cédric explained that everything had come to a head during his nephew's 30th birthday. He had called at the house to collect a small present and share a cake that she'd baked him. His father had returned in a filthy mood and reeking of drink; aggressive and argumentative. He'd berated Cédric's sister for the money spent on his son's gift and had accused her of pampering him like a kid once he'd caught sight of the cake. He'd picked it up and thrown it at her causing the whipped cream to cover her face and the cake to fall to the kitchen floor. He had then delivered a punch to his wife's stomach which had sent her reeling into a cupboard and knocked her to the floor. Cédric paused as he thought of his sister's gentle demeanour and how difficult these brutal outbursts must have been for her. Lottie held his hand as he persevered with the explanation. The drunken slob had continued kicking her, calling her names and berating her as he shouted that she was good for nothing other than spending his money. She'd curled herself into a ball to protect her face as she'd done so many times before whilst Jean-Louis had looked on in horror telling his father to stop and it was just a cake that had cost her a few euros to make. On that day Jean-Louis had really believed his father might kill his mother and all because of him. Yet again there had been no rhyme or reason to his father's anger as he continued to lash out with his feet. When he had pulled his wife up from the floor and started to hit her repeatedly around the face, his nephew had realised that he needed to act. His dad had always kept his mother's face clear of bruises in order there was no evidence of his assaults but that particular day had been different and his father was like a crazed animal. Convinced he had to stop his father from killing his mother, he had opened the kitchen drawer and found a carving knife which he'd plunged into his father's back. At that point the kicking stopped and the full horror of what he'd done engulfed his nephew.

His mother, still dazed, hadn't fully comprehended what had just taken place other than seeing her husband's prostate body lying next to her. She'd allowed Jean-Louis to pick her up, take her into the sitting room and make her a hot drink. He'd ensured she didn't have any pains that were out of the ordinary for a beating and then gone back to the kitchen to telephone the police. Even with mitigating circumstances and an understanding judge, his nephew couldn't escape a prison term and he'd found himself sentenced to five years. Cédric knew little of his nephew's life in the penitentiary other than he'd spent much of his time studying and that he'd managed to stay out of the day-to-day fights incited by some of the inmates.

When he eventually got parole, he had found it hard to find work as nobody was interested in someone who had been in gaol and the stigma followed behind Jean-Louis like the grim reaper. Cédric's sister had died of cancer four years ago and he'd been surprised, if not delighted, when his nephew had arrived at the funeral declaring he had "found God" and was a member of an abbey a couple of hours' drive from Cédric's home. Over the next few weeks, Cédric had learned a little more about Brother Jean-Louis Pislait's role managing the importation of ecclesiastical works that were resold to interested parties. It had been Cédric's idea to help cost the leather books for resale as Jean-Louis had no idea what value to put on the items. The elderly man stopped talking and looked at her wondering how she would judge him and this young man with all his problems. Lottie acknowledged the nephew's life had been derailed from the start and that he appeared to have overcome his battles in later life when he found the abbey. She hoped that Cédric could take some comfort from those later years even though she couldn't alter her opinion of the nephew.

As he spoke of Jean-Louis, she found herself wondering about the connection with the monk who had been following him who had been on his mobile phone. Had Cedric's nephew committed suicide or was the monk involved in his death? She made them both a fresh drink and listened to him explaining the funeral plans that were now in progress following the autopsy. He would scatter his ashes, as he had done for his sibling, and mother and son would be together again which was his only solace. Lottie eventually made her excuses and put on her coat to return to the apartment. Although she didn't really know Cédric Mallet and she knew to be careful when addressing elderly people which required the "*vous*" format of you and not "*tu*", she decided to kiss him gently before leaving. He patted her hand repeatedly thanking her for coming to talk to him.

Lottie headed out into the corridor and was just passing a noticeboard headed "Événements Futurs" with the home's future activities when she spotted him in the distance signing into the register. She stopped in her tracks, looking left and right, as she considered somewhere suitable to hide. At the desk was the monk and everything about him, the black robe, his height and weight, all indicated that this was the man who had been following Jean-Louis before his death. This was not a person that Lottie wanted to encounter. She shot down a corridor where she came upon a generously proportioned woman pushing a lunch trolley stacked with plates and metal covers. She smiled at her weakly and headed down the corridor as if she knew exactly where she was going. She then double-backed and tucked herself behind the wide–bottomed woman as she swung around the corner and headed up the corridor. As the monk passed the lunch trolley, Lottie tucked in between the trolley and the wall just as the woman was starting to ask Lottie what the hell she was doing. She smiled apologetically and glanced back in time to see the monk knocking on Cédric's door.

As she drove home, she speculated whether the eighty-year-old could be involved in some way with recent events. He seemed genuinely distressed at the loss of Jean-Louis but why would the monk have reason to visit him? How well did Cédric know the monk? She berated herself for not checking his name in the Visitors' Book but her only thought was to put as much distance between her and the person in the religious attire. When she got back to the apartment, she decided to ring "worst case" to let her know the monk had been at the retirement home and she'd seen him knocking on the uncle's door. Lepireon thanked her for the information and advised she would follow up with the retirement home but declined, or refused, to comment on Lottie's questions regarding progress on Jean-Louis Pislait's death.

Lottie wasn't sure she'd hear anything more on the incident and put it out of her mind. That was until the morning when she received a phone call from the television company. The black and red book was being used as an action prop, therefore, it was an active part in the storyline in which one of the actors had to periodically pick it up, read it or throw it onto a table as part of his role. The Floor Manager advised the pages in the book were becoming detached and did she have a restorer as there were a number of weeks still to run before the programme would end production. Lottie wondered if Cédric Mallet might be willing to do a repair although she wasn't exactly ecstatic at the idea of returning to the home even if Monsieur Mallet was a total sweetie.

She confirmed that they would need to drop off the book before Friday and she'd do her best even though she couldn't promise a professional repair. The damaged book was duly delivered on Wednesday morning and, in the evening, Lottie drove to the retirement home to check whether Cédric could restore it. She signed in and did her best to surreptitiously peel back the pages by a few days to try and identify the name of the monk. She was even prepared to take a photo of the page on her mobile phone as she'd seen in television dramas, however, she hadn't anticipated the member of staff refreshing the flowers in the entrance area. She had to ditch her plan and instead signed her name, the date and time, and who she was visiting. Perhaps she'd get lucky when she left?

Cédric was delighted to see her and this time they exchanged polite kisses rather than a formal handshake. He hustled her into the room whilst reciting a selection of the teas he could offer her: mint, jasmine, *thé vert*, various individual fruits or maybe one of the mixed combinations? Lottie opted for a thyme and lemon tea and reached in her bag for the packet of Breton *gallette* biscuits that she'd bought before arriving at the home. All elderly people liked sweet things and she'd eyed a packet of "*petit beurre*" last time she was in his room. She also took the book out of her briefcase and let him examine why the pages were lifting from the spine. He confirmed that his arthritis would affect his ability to manipulate the leather but he still thought he could repair it. He had brought some of his tools with him as he couldn't bear to part with them. Every resident had brought a variety of personal effects and he hoped he might be useful if any repairs were required.

Cédric put the book to one side and focused on making the tea. Lottie suggested that she come back at the weekend if he thought that would be enough time thereby inducing a cynical response in English of "what else do I have to occupy my days Madame Pearce?" There was little she could do other than agree that retirement could sometimes be complicated. Lottie fluctuated back and forth on whether she should ask about the monk's visit until she blurted it out so there was no way back. Cédric said the monk was his nephew's work colleague at the abbey and he'd confirmed the books were extremely popular amongst the private collectors and the galleries. His nephew's comrade wanted to ensure Cédric could continue receiving the shipments and offer his invaluable advice and recommendations on price. In the light of Cédric's earlier remark, Lottie recognised how this role gave him a sense of purpose and she pressed on with her quest by asking the monk's name. Cédric wasn't too sure he'd told him and the more he stressed about his memory, the more he realised that the man had only introduced himself as Jean-Louis' friend at the abbey. Lottie knew it must be true as he was as sharp as a needle and there was nothing wrong with his memory. She recalled his structured list of furniture and the detailed measurements he'd provided before the move into the residential home. He might have fewer years to live than he had already lived but there was not a sniff of dementia or any other mental decline.

They chatted easily as Lottie explained her children's jobs and personalities, Bob's death, her move to France and her new life in Avignon. Cédric, who was clearly enjoying her company, occasionally dropped in an English sentence which was sometimes no longer grammatically perfect but was delivered with such a superb accent that Lottie commended him; his eyes twinkled and shone as he recalled his years with Renault. Eventually, she realised that the daylight was fading and she was just about to say her farewells when there was a knock at the door. She found herself once more in front of the lady whose ample proportions had provided a suitable barrier from the monk spotting her in the corridor. She was bringing Cédric's evening meal even though he could have eaten in the public dining room in the company of other inmates. Cédric far preferred his own room to the public spaces choosing only to use them when he wanted to read a newspaper or magazine thus compelling him to pop into the public rooms every morning to check if they'd been delivered. Lottie said her goodbyes and set off home as her own stomach was rumbling even though the canteen smell emanating from his dinner tray did not suggest *haute cuisine*. It was only when she was heading over the bridge that she remembered she'd not checked the Visitors' Book to identify the name of the monk. "Damn and blast - *tête de linotte* Lottie" she uttered audibly acknowledging her scatterbrain to herself.

As it was Francine's shift at the *brocante* the next day, she had a long lie-in and indulged herself by spending the time in a comfy, hyacinth blue lounger with an elastic waist.

79

After she'd done an hour of paperwork, she curled up on the settee with her antique books and spent a lovely day listening to music and relaxing. She switched off the bedside lamp after a thoroughly indulgent few hours and, in those twilight moments before sleep, she congratulated herself on her move to France and her new life. It had been a huge risk and Pislait's death had caused a serious wobble to her plan and yet she'd never been happier even though Bob was not lying alongside her.

In the morning Lottie dressed and prepared to do a weekend shop at the *Auchan* supermarket. She needed to pop over to Villeneuve to collect the book from Cédric and she also wanted to explore other baby shops to get a little something for Regina who now went under the handle of "Gigi". She grabbed a selection of carrier bags and headed to the Renault estate. It was parked in her assigned space; each apartment in the building had a brass plate identifying two spaces per flat number. She thought the car looked different in some way but didn't immediately understand why until she reached it and saw that all four tyres were flat. One tyre would have been frustrating and irritating but four! She began to wonder if she'd run over something the night before that would cause the tyre problem but then she spotted a note flapping on her windscreen.

"Rendez les livres immédiatement. La prochaine fois, ce ne sera pas votre voiture!" She considered the note demanding the immediate return of the books and that next time it would not be her car that was damaged. Her stomach lurched as she considered the threat and realised that the perpetrator knew where she lived. The demands had escalated and her property had now been violated. She genuinely feared that she might be attacked or be the next "Jean-Louis". She decided to contact "worst case" and

was advised that she was not at the station but would be returning at the end of the morning. The brigadier on the phone would pass a text message to her immediately. Lottie had realised the cost of the four tyres would be more than the excess on her insurance so she requested "worst case" call her back with a case number that she could use for an insurance claim. She walked back into the apartment as the urgency of shopping and other frivolous activities dissolved with her growing sense of dread that she was being watched.

She made herself a coffee and had just sat down when the hyper efficient Brigadier-Chef rang her back. She advised she was only ten minutes away and she'd call in at her apartment if Lottie could remind her of the address. Lepireon arrived with two other officers who deferred to her as the senior member of the team. Lepireon and Lottie walked into the apartment leaving the two men to check over the car. They checked for fingerprints on the chassis and the tyres but nothing was evident other than noting the tyres had been slashed with a knife. Lepireon confirmed the person would have, undoubtedly, worn gloves causing Lottie to voice her fears that this was all related to Jean-Louis, the monk and the books as she showed her the note that had been on the windscreen. One of the team, now back in her flat, dug into their back pocket for a pair of latex gloves and took it from her. He brushed an adhesive powder across the paper and there were a couple of prints visible front and back on the paper but Lottie accepted that they were probably hers. Lepireon asked her to call into the station tomorrow so they could take her fingerprints and eliminate her from the evidence on the note. They were heading back to the police station after seeing her, so Lottie asked for a lift given that lack of transport was a problem and there was no immediate timeline for the car to be fixed.

The attack on the car was stomach-churning and swiftly becoming the only priority of the day.

If the fear had not been so all encompassing, she could have laughed at her trip in the white and blue *Police Municipale* vehicle where she sat in the rear seat with one of the officers and peered out at people going about their everyday business. To the unknown eye, she looked like she'd been picked up by them and was heading off to be questioned at the "nick" but in truth she was only too happy to be in their company and. if the "tyre slasher" was watching, then so much the better.

Once at the police headquarters, her fingerprints were taken and she completed the paperwork to ensure she had a claim number for the insurance company whom she rang whilst still at the station. They were extremely efficient in confirming they would contact "*Point S*", the local tyre dealers, who would come to the apartment before the end of the day to fit replacement tyres to her vehicle. Lottie decided to get a taxi back to the flat as this was not the moment to be searching for bus timetables and she needed to quell the alarm that was growing as she considered when and how this book nightmare might end. From the apartment, she rang Philippe and updated him on the latest incident. He was equally surprised that her car had been vandalised at her home address and listened as Lottie explained the content of the note on the windscreen. He instructed her to ring the television company immediately and to get the books back so that at least they were in her possession as and when future contact would be made. Lottie hadn't truly considered the possibility of further contact and had concentrated only on the warning aspect of the message. Philippe was right, how would they get the books if she didn't get them back? She explained to

Philippe that one was with Cédric and she was collecting it later that evening resulting in him suggesting an evening meal at a restaurant in Avignon. Lottie really didn't feel like being sociable and preferred to sign off acknowledging she'd ring him tomorrow.

She made a cup of tea and sank into the settee trying to prevent her head from imagining all manner of horrifying scenarios. The phone rang and she hoped it was *"Point S"* so she'd have her car up and running again and be self-sufficient. It was Cédric Mallet and he sounded hysterical. He was talking so fast that he sounded like a machine gun firing words like multiple rounds of bullets. Lottie could only catch one word in ten so in a calm voice she asked him to stop, to speak slowly and to start again from the beginning.

He took a deep breath and explained more calmly that he was now working on the book as he had been unwell yesterday, so he had only just started to repair it. In order to reset the pages and to restore the book, he had removed it from the tooled leather cover so he could work on the spine. In doing so, the spine itself was a solid block of beige powder in a plastic liner. He had a sinking feeling it was some sort of narcotic but he could not imagine his nephew would have known anything about it as he was just responsible for bringing them to Cédric to be priced. Lottie listened and spent several minutes placating the agitated man and then advised she had no car until the end of the day. She would come over in the evening and collect the book and take it to the *Police Municipale*. She did not want to mention about his nephew following her, or the damage to her car, or the threatening note. What possible advantage could there be for Cédric to be party to all this upsetting news?

She rang "worst case" again and updated her of Monsieur Mallet's discovery. She advised that she would prefer Lottie not to collect the book on her own and that they could go together to his residential home. That seemed a better idea and Lottie felt comforted that she no longer had to take responsibility for the book. It was an uncomfortable afternoon trapped in the flat with an over creative imagination which threw up no end of alarming scenarios. The only interruption was "Point S" who arrived to remove and replace the damaged tyres. Lottie couldn't muster up the energy to explain how she'd got the four flats preferring to let the two men imagine she'd had a fight with a boyfriend or a husband. It was all too much and just easier to let them make up their own minds about the story behind the repairs.

Fortunately, Lepireon didn't arrive until the Renault was back in one piece, so she was able to go to the residential home with them and took up her position in the back of the police car. A man accompanying "worst case" was introduced as Capitaine Lebrun, a crime investigator with the *Police Judiciaire*; part of the *Police Nationale*. Lottie found the French police system very confusing. She knew the difference between the *gendarmes* and the *police municipale* as they wore different uniforms and drove vehicles in different colours and logos. The *gendarmes* were trained as part of the French armed forces and were evident in the small villages and towns whilst also having a military defence function. She knew the *gendarmes* were under the administration of the Ministry of Defence whereas the *Police Municipale* reported to the city Mayor. She thought she remembered that the *Police Nationale* reported to the Ministry of the Interior but she couldn't recall the ins and outs of France's confusing system. It made the police structure in the UK seem like a walk in the park as each of the French brigades seem to have their own hierarchical structure and job titles, plus differing pips, stripes and other insignia denoting their status.

On hearing the name of Capitaine Lebrun, Lottie had to stifle a giggle as she immediately thought of being curled up with Bob on the settee in Marlow watching the old "Maigret" programmes. Wasn't he called *Capitaine* or was it *Commissaire Maigret*? She couldn't recall but she remembered the wonderful images of Paris and that he worked in the *Sûreté*. As with many things, the *Sûreté* no longer existed and had been renamed *Police Nationale* but Lottie was oblivious to the rebranding. She presumed the man in front of her must be the equivalent of a detective and she addressed both of them explaining that she had not mentioned to Cédric about Jean-Louis' pursuit of her along Rue de la République. Monsieur Mallet also had no knowledge of the attack on her car and she really didn't want to alarm him given he was eighty years of age. He might be stressed by the contents hidden in the spine of the book but perhaps he could be spared other details if they were in agreement. They concurred that it was not the time to disclose any suspicions surrounding Jean-Louis' demise or the vandalism of her car.

The residential home's Duty Manager was naturally extremely perturbed to have a *Police Municipale* car pull up in front of their reception. She came out to welcome the visitors and raised both eyebrows at the mention of them needing to talk to Cédric Mallet whom she considered a gentle and insular man who rarely came out of his room other than to sit in the garden or read his newspaper in the lounge. She accompanied them to the door but was diplomatically discharged from any further involvement as Lepireon knocked on it. She headed back to her office wondering what the hell this considerate man could have done to demand a visit from the police and she checked the name and rank of the man with the Brigadier-Chef who had introduced himself on arrival. The troop entered Cédric's room where he did a double take at Lepireon in her police uniform and accompanied by a man whom he did not know. He took Lottie's hand and she could feel his own trembling as he asked them all to take a seat. He produced the book which was no longer intact and explained how he had come across the plastic sleeve running full length down the spine. They looked over the remnants of the book and then at the slab of beige powder from which they removed a few granules and placed them in a separate bag. The senior officer added a solution and agitated the bag whereupon it turned blue and Lottie caught the look that passed between them. They took Cédric's fingerprints explaining the bag contained narcotics and they would need to eliminate his own traces on the bag and the book. Cédric's head was full of questions which they did their best to answer without stressing the elderly man too much. He advised there was another delivery scheduled for tomorrow which had surprised him as there was usually a gap of a few weeks between them. He didn't know anything more other than the monk would contact him to arrange collection so what should he do? "Worst case" told him to ring her the moment that the books arrived and that he was not to contact the monk. Cédric confirmed that he couldn't call him as he had no information about the man and didn't even know his name.

Lottie felt very worried as they made their farewells and the sweet-tempered pensioner was left alone in his room with just his thoughts and fears. He'd made the discovery which they confirmed was a narcotic but they wouldn't explain much more. Before leaving the residential home, "worst case" checked the Visitors' Book on the day that Lottie had visited the home and seen the monk. The ledger confirmed he was called Brother Michel Vialat. As they all drove back to Lottie's apartment, the detective confirmed that he would need the name of the television company that was holding the remaining books and that he would need to impound them immediately. She confirmed that she had all the relevant information back at the apartment.

Once they were back in the city centre, Lottie booted up her laptop and also dug out the signed contract. They took copies of the document via their mobile phones and she had to forward the other details via email. Lepireon advised they would have a patrol unit situated outside the gates of the *Hotel Particulier* as the findings from the powder, combined with the tyre incident, were of sufficient concern that there was now a level of escalation in reclaiming the books. Lottie contemplated how understated she made it all sound. She asked if she would be allowed to spend the night elsewhere and they acknowledged it was advisable. She decided to ring Philippe to see if he had a spare room even though she knew little about him other than his caring manner after Pislait's death; she assumed he lived in Avignon. He was delighted to receive her call and was only too pleased to be her knight in shining armour or, as he called it, "*chevalier servant*". He said he'd come and collect her but for some reason, Lottie preferred to drive and noted down his address. She put a few things in a bag and headed towards the car just as a patrol vehicle parked up alongside the gates. She stopped to let them know she was going to the home of Philippe Percey and gave them his address. Having punched the details into her own GPS, she was surprised to find it was only ten minutes from her; allowing for not getting lost and finding a parking space.

She had no idea if he had a garage which were always gold dust in any city.

CHAPTER FIVE
A COMFORTING SHOULDER

Once she'd arrived in front of a bungalow with a letterbox announcing PERCEY Philippe, he ran out and invited her to park in the garage alongside his jeep. He kissed her fervently and enveloped her in his firm, athletic arms. Tucking his arm through hers, he exclaimed "*Entrez, ma chère*". He showed her to the guest bedroom with its en suite bathroom and left her to settle herself whilst he went to open a bottle of white wine. Lottie took in her surroundings which had a surprisingly feminine touch. She set out her toiletries in the bathroom and then walked down to the corridor where she could hear noises emanating from what might be the kitchen. Philippe was pulling a cork from the bottle and bemoaning that it was plastic and not the natural product from a tree. He poured the light, crisp wine into two elegant crystal glasses and passed one to her. She took a hefty swig rather than a small sip and exhaled with such force that he looked at her sympathetically as his face acknowledged it had been a hell of a day.

Philippe directed her through to the sitting room where jazz music was playing from an MP3 player set in a docking station. Bob and Lottie's love of jazz had caused her to bring a host of CDs to France that they'd collected over the years rather than leave them for the Cadougans. He sat her down and asked her to recount the events since the death of Jean-Louis but only if she felt able to relive it all again. She picked her way through the nightmare from almost bumping into the monk at the home, the tyres, the confirmation of narcotics in the spine of the book and the patrol car now parked outside her home. Philippe studied her earnestly as she brought him up to date. He asked what was happening with the other books and she confirmed the police were going to request them from the production company which he confirmed made sense as someone clearly wanted them back at any cost. He asked what the drug was in the book, however, Lottie didn't know as the police had only confirmed "narcotics". She contemplated why he wanted to know and, once more, wondered how disassociated he might be from the book fiasco.

When they'd sunk a half bottle of the wine and Lottie was feeling considerably more relaxed, he suggested they go to a local restaurant for dinner but Lottie asked if he had any food in the house or maybe they could get a takeaway? She really didn't feel like sitting through a formal or informal meal with a sea of faces she didn't know. He suggested knocking up a fresh basil, tomato and chilli pasta and she instantly leapt on the proposition. He poured her another glass and invited her to relax as he'd go and raid the fridge. Lottie kicked off her shoes and curled her legs up under her on the settee. This was lovely, this was what she needed. Thank God for Philippe.

When she'd reached the end of her wine, she popped into the kitchen to see if she could help him. As she turned the corner, she saw Philippe on his phone and he coloured up in discomfort, dropping the phone onto the worktop, as he set about chopping some tomatoes. Lottie didn't know what to make of his lack of composure and found herself wondering who had been on the phone and what he had been saying to them? In a wine befuddled haze, she found herself automatically pulling herself together and her brain confirmed that she needed to stay on her guard. She really liked him but there seemed to be threats all around her nowadays causing a mistrust that could spoil their evening. Even with her anxiety and concerns in overdrive, she couldn't help herself from laughing and joking as they prepared garlic bread together making all the usual jokes about not kissing anyone. She found him funny and charismatic as he showed her how to remove the greenish centre of the fresh clove and explained it was the villain that produced the garlicky bad breath. She made a mental note as cooking with garlic was the French equivalent of butter in the UK so few recipes existed without it.

They had a lovely meal accompanied by another bottle of wine but this time it was a Rhône red. After the pasta, Philippe put together a small cheeseboard with a loaf of healthy, brown bread known as "*complet*". As they sat back down on the settee for coffee, it was not a huge surprise that Philippe moved in to kiss her. She had already considered he might make a move whilst they'd been eating and had found herself considering how Bob would react if she was unfaithful to him. She wasn't ready to explore any new relationships even following her husband's monstrous deceit about his daughter, Fleur. Lottie withdrew rapidly from his advance causing Philippe's cheeks to radiate once more with embarrassment. He fell over himself apologising and calling himself stupid, "*un idiot*" and was utterly mortified. Lottie felt uncomfortable explaining she was just tired by all that had occurred and she was also sorry but her head was all over the place or, as she expressed it, "*ma tête est partout*". Philippe readily accepted this and changed the conversation to talk of the *brocante*, her flat, her UK family and Lottie asked more about Philippe and his daughter, Natalie, from his former marriage. They charged through each subject trying to recapture the light atmosphere that had prevailed in the kitchen and at the table. By midnight, Lottie could no longer mask the yawns and they both retired to their bedrooms where Lottie lay awake and tossed and turned for at least an hour. She had no idea what was in Philippe's head as he lay in his bed further along the corridor.

The following morning Lottie woke early and reflected on a lovely meal with Philippe who was undeniably great company even though her antennae were still warning her to maintain a distance. He'd made a clumsy, amorous pass as she was battling with her feelings versus the importance of safeguarding herself. Eventually, she detected movement so sprang out of bed and into the bathroom. Once dressed, she joined him in the kitchen as he prepared their breakfast and she breathed in the fragrance of fresh, roasted coffee. He was laying a table with plates and two large blue bowls which sat alongside fresh rolls, buttery croissants and three small pots of jam. She asked if she could help but he gently pecked her on both cheeks and confirmed it was all under control. They sat in silence munching on the rolls and slurping from the two large bowls of coffee. She still couldn't break the lifelong habit of using a mug, however, it was clear the body dehydrated overnight and a bowl made a lot more sense. He asked her plans for the day and for the weekend in an attempt to rebuild the companionship that had been paralysed by his clumsy move. She'd lost track that it was Saturday morning, so she revisited the idea of checking out the baby shops in Avignon or perhaps a drive down to the vast shopping estate at Le Pontet. The daylight made her feel stronger and she advised she would return to the apartment after shopping. Even though he looked disappointed at her plan, he assured her of a continued safe haven at his home, no matter the hour or day.

Lottie set off for the flat and was relieved to find a different patrol car sitting outside the gates. She waved to them and they acknowledged her return. She unpacked her overnight bag, checked through some post and, once more, got her carrier bags together and headed out of the building. When her mobile rang, she could see the incoming call was from the designer at the television company. He was ringing to check if she had any other books as the three remaining books had been taken overnight by the police and he was extremely frustrated at losing part of his set design and the red book that was an integral prop to the action. He asked in the politest of terms "what the hell's going on?" Lottie's theatre days enabled her to comprehend his total frustration even though a theatre had greater flexibility as there were no continuity issues on how sets appeared from one performance to the next. She confirmed that she did not have access to any more of the beautiful leather-bound books and she was extremely apologetic for the inconvenience and all the problems that the loss must be causing the production team. She didn't feel she could explain why the books had been impounded and hoped the police had provided a prudent explanation.

She tried to explain the role of a prop maker in Britain. When she didn't know a particular word in French, she spent ages constructing lengthy sentences until hopefully the person understood what she was trying to communicate. She tried the same system asking if they had a supplier who made replica items. The Production Designer did not respond so she carried on with her description of a company who made replica items or ad hoc requests for over-sized or under-sized items and who worked with latex, fibreglass, metal, fabrics, etc. She continued that the items they made were not *"effets spéciaux"* and he cut across her stating in English how could they be "special effects" as they were simply books. She observed a decent English accent and wondered if the role was the same so repeated the need for a Prop Maker, a Prop Builder, an artisan who could remake a copy from images that they would hopefully have on file.

It became clear that he had grasped what she was trying to say and also that no more books would be available to the production. He was extremely dissatisfied and frustrated stating the company would never use her again. At the thought of losing their business, her first rental to a television company, she decided to come clean even it invoked the wrath of the police. She explained that the books contained some sort of narcotic in the spine which was completely unknown to her or the person who sold them to her. Lottie felt pretty certain Cédric was above suspicion; Jean-Louis perhaps not so much. The phone line went quiet as the designer absorbed the facts surrounding the missing books. He apologised for verbally attacking her and adding to her problems as he now understood why the books had been seized and would transmit the details to the team. Lottie wondered if she would now have "worst case" on her back. How many monkeys can one person support?

She sank into the car feeling despondent and angry with the world. She drove out onto the main road deciding she'd go to the shopping estate and she'd call back at *Auchan* supermarket on her return. She wasn't in the best frame of mind but maybe looking at clothes for new-born babies would cheer her up. Fortunately, this proved to be the case as she found a delectable floral jumpsuit with matching headband and waited patiently whilst the item was wrapped so beautifully that it looked like a work of art and at no extra cost. She made a mental note to always reply "*oui*" if someone said "*c'est un cadeau, Madame?*"

Cédric rang her around 11h30 to confirm the books had arrived and that, surprisingly, the courier said there was another delivery clearing customs and he'd be back on Monday morning. He'd never, ever,
 had shipments back-to-back. The deliveries were usually weeks apart and he didn't understand why a system that had operated so well with Jean-Louis was now so different. He confirmed the policewoman had collected the morning delivery of books and he'd notified her of the Monday delivery. Lepireon had told him not to worry and he was to do the same procedure of contacting her when they arrived. Lottie could hear the anguish in his voice as he recounted the news of a further shipment and she did her best to console him. He was extremely worried that the monk would be back in touch as he'd be wanting to collect the additional shipment. "*Aller voir le gestionnaire et lui dire de bloquer les appels et les visiteurs car tu ne te sentes pas bien*" she instructed her agitated friend. Cédric giggled nervously and declared she had a dishonest streak in her that he'd need to watch as asking the manager to block his calls and visitors was a capital idea. He hung up still chuckling at Lottie's response.

Cédric Mallet was not convinced his acting skills were up to the job in hand and speculated if his heart was up to all this lying and skulduggery. The weekend could not pass quickly enough as he wished away his life even though each day was precious at his age. Monday eventually arrived together with the second delivery by the courier company. For the moment he had avoided any contact from the abbey but now he was supposedly holding two consignments and they must be in contact soon; it was only a matter of when.

The policewoman returned to collect the second delivery and he was astonished to find her holding the shipment of less ornate books that had been delivered on Saturday. She explained that the books had undergone thorough testing and they were clean. Given the abbey might be in contact, she was giving him back Saturday's consignment so he could pass them over to Brother Vialat. She gave him the books in their original box and advised Cédric to deny receiving any other shipments since this one. He tried to explain that his lies might not be convincing and he no longer wanted to be part of this unfolding horror story. He'd begun to wonder if his nephew, Jean-Louis, had died from an unfortunate accident or if there was more to it. Lepireon stayed long enough to convince him that he was integral to resolving the crime and his assistance formed a key role in bringing the perpetrators to justice. Cédric Mallet found himself unable to challenge this tenet.

Lottie was relieved to have the distraction of the *brocante* on Monday. She went down to the workshop as Francine had taken delivery of a 1930's settee with two armchairs on Friday. She was excited to see the design, the condition of the items and delighted that the temporary Edwardian settee and armchairs could be removed from the Art Nouveau/Art Deco living room and returned to their original location. Lottie clapped her hands in ecstasy as she looked at the vibrant green suite with its hexagonal design woven into the green fabric. The lines were typically clean, simple and understated. The condition of the armchairs was just as good as the state of the settee and she wondered how Francine had heard about the furniture and what type of home they had been sitting in to have been treated so well. Alain agreed with her and pointed out that Madame Besnier had also acquired two side tables in the same collection. They were all fine specimens and they both walked to the 1930s room holding a side table. Lottie explained where to put the furniture and where to relocate the Edwardian suite.

She knew Alain had a kettle in his workshop but she chose to invite him up to the office to share a coffee with her. He was a hard worker and needed little to no daily instruction and it was about time she got to know him a bit better. Slowly, bit by bit, she was starting to learn about the individuals who made up the team. She'd noted all the names of the craftsmen and craftswomen that Mimi had listed during the transfer, together with notes on their particular traits and characteristics. She had explained exactly what items were with each of the artisans so she could justifiably contact them some weeks later to introduce herself, check on progress, and ask when the items might be returned. They all sounded a positive bunch and she only had one or two who might need a weekly call to chase for the finished goods.

There were two carpenters who shared the furniture workload; naturally there was Philippe who was particularly skilled at marquetry and inlay and who was swiftly becoming equally important as a confidante and a comforting shoulder to lean upon. The other cabinetmaker was Claire; a great all-rounder who could add a replacement foot to a wardrobe and make it look like it had been there for fifty years. The mechanical brains of the outfit responsible for automatons, watches, clocks, grandfather clocks and anything that had cogs, wheels and gears or mini motors was Gilles. Any delicate china or porcelain items came under the direction of Fifi who could make cracks and chips vanish in a puff of smoke like a skilful magician. The only married team were Chantal and Allesandro Rossi who had responsibility for silverware and were related to Renzo who handled any reframing and restoration of paintings and other artwork. There were still one or two artisans whom she had not met. The metal worker, Lucas, and the glass worker, Mathilde, sprang to mind and she decided to contact them to make an appointment to say "hello" even if they were not working on any of the emporium's items just now.

The part-time contract with Alain was a huge relief to Lottie as there seemed to be a constant turnaround of goods; those that were coming in as stock and those sold to the clients. He was a competent lad who was often willing to work a bit of overtime for cash when the official twenty hours were exceeded. Lottie invited him to leave the side tables that he was still moving around the 1930s sitting room and come and join her for a coffee which should be ready by now. He cheerfully accepted the offer of Lottie's machine rather than the one in his workshop which periodically dispensed a brown sludge across his bench. He was standing in Reception chatting happily with her and clutching his small white cup when the monk arrived, slamming the door behind him and making Alain jump and spill his drink on some papers on the desk.

Lottie looked up in alarm as the door slammed and was about to say *"Attention de la porte s'il vous plaît"* when her eyes fell upon the black habit with the cowl still raised up over his head. She was very glad to have Alain alongside her even though he would have no idea who the monk was or what he wanted. There was no escaping a confrontation and Lottie realised she didn't mind as the monk needed to understand she was no longer in possession of the books.

She pushed the equivalent of a steel pole up the back of her spine and stepped towards him deciding that, if she took the initiative, she might feel less intimidated. She looked him straight in the eyes whilst striving to create a photographic image of his face in her brain. She asked how she could help him and waited for the reply as it was clear he was not dropping into the *brocante* to buy a table or a painting. It was no surprise that he demanded the return of the books purchased from Cédric Mallet. Lottie addressed him in a clipped tone acknowledging the books were neither in her possession nor were they with the theatre company. She remembered that he thought it was a theatre group, so she added the erroneous information just for good measure. Naturally, this led to him to challenge who had them. She uttered four words *"Le Police Municipale Monsieur"*. She sensed Alain's eyes were now popping out of their sockets. He knew Madame Pearce to be a gentle and kind lady but she seemed to have transformed into a steely matron reprimanding a small kid – well worse because this was a man of the cloth and she didn't seem to be showing him any respect whatsoever.

At Lottie's disclosure that the books were with the police, the monk's assertive and threatening manner underwent a slight modification as he stared fixedly at her. She could sense his brain computing her response and its consequences. *"Une grave erreur, Madame Pearce"* he uttered before turning heel, opening the door and disappearing across the courtyard. Lottie flopped down into her chair after the confrontation and could feel Alain's eyes burning through the top of her head. She was relieved Brother Vialat knew she no longer had the books even if he deemed it "a serious error" that they were with the police. She didn't trust herself to explain anything to Alain who was looking at her in total shock and uttering *"ça va Madame*

Pearce?" She confirmed that she was OK and there'd been a problem with some books which the police had confiscated. Whether out of politeness or respect, he chose not to prod further but he was pretty curious to know who the monk was and why his boss was clearly alarmed and frightened to see him. He got them both a top up from the coffee machine and returned to the workshop scratching his head in bewilderment.

Lottie spent the next few minutes checking the camera footage on her laptop and was delighted to see a perfectly sharp image of Brother Michel Vialat looking back at her. She picked up the phone to contact "worst case". Lottie explained the monk's facial features; the green eyes, aquiline face and slightly beaky nose. His eyelashes and eyebrows were a sandy colour but she'd not seen any sign of his hair – perhaps it was shaved or he was bald? Brigadier-Chef Lepireon explained how to take a screenshot of the image on the security footage and asked her to email it to her. Lottie took the opportunity to enquire after the two shipments of books they'd collected from Cédric and whether or not they contained drugs. "Worst case" didn't seem forthcoming about sharing any information, so she declared she was very worried about Cédric and his mental state following recent events. Lepireon relented and advised that a consignment he had received a few days ago was surprisingly drug-free but the further shipment, which had arrived within 48 hours, did contain narcotics in the spines of a further 6 books. Whatever the reason for the innocuous shipment, they were still conducting their investigations and she was pretty certain no further shipments would be delivered to Monsieur Mallet given Madame Pearce had now informed the messenger, Brother Vialat, that the police were involved and had impounded the items.

She agreed with her that it was highly unlikely there would be more shipments and asked whether she could update Cédric to lessen his anxiety. Lepireon concurred as the force had not been back in touch with him since collecting the latest delivery of six books even though he knew one delivery was drug-free. Just before putting the phone down, Lottie attempted one more question when she queried what drugs were packed in the spines. She got a one word reply of "*cocaïne*" and heard the click of the line as Lepireon ended the call.

Lottie replaced the receiver and found she was shivering. She suddenly felt really cold and presumed it must be shock brought on by the recent visitor together with Lepireon's news. She had been warned off by a monk who seemed to double as a drug dealer and started to comprehend the considerable danger of the last few weeks. She got up to make yet another coffee or maybe a tisane so she'd not be too wired for the rest of the day.

Lottie called into a bakery on her way home and bought a couple of appetising tarts piled high with fresh fruits and sitting on top of a confectioner's custard base. She had no gym membership yet in France but her weight seemed to have stayed the same or perhaps it had even reduced from all the stress. There was certainly a promising amount of flexibility on her skirt waistbands as she deliberated the benefits of a Mediterranean diet. She drove to Cédric's feeling upbeat and relieved that life seemed to be back to some form of "normal". She was pleased to find him sitting out in the garden in a comfy deckchair with a newspaper at his feet and a rug around his legs. She approached quietly, as he appeared to be asleep, yet within seconds he sat up bolt upright sensing her approach - clearly his hearing was as sharp as the day he was born. She grinned warmly at him and jiggled the box slightly announcing "*gateaux*". He grinned at her as she helped him gather up his affairs and they walked back to his room to prepare a drink. The evening air had cooled and it was time to turn in.

Lottie would have preferred a cup of Earl Grey or Darjeeling tea rather than a fruit tisane but the French were not into tea with milk so she accepted a camomile in the hope it would "work" with the fruit tart. She updated him on the encounter with the monk at the *brocante* and made certain she included Alain in the description so he was not anxious that she'd been alone. He was relieved to know that Jean-Louis' supposed friend now recognised that she no longer had the books. He presumed, no he hoped, that this must mean Brother Vialat also realised he no longer had any books awaiting collection. He wasn't sure the monk would put all the pieces together to accept that the police had taken his latest consignment and Lottie could sense the cogs whirring as he pieced together the information. She suggested that he did exactly as before and ask the staff to intercept and block any visitors or calls – except hers or the police!

CHAPTER SIX
SEEK AND YOU SHALL FIND

With matters nicely tucked up and being handled by the police, Lottie returned her full focus to the *brocante* and growing the stock. She was delighted that sales had stayed strong following the change in ownership. Mimi had provided the last year's sales figures as part of the data that Lottie and her brother had reviewed back in the UK. Even without rentals, the business usually grew year on year and the initial signs supported an upward trend which she would need to monitor if her new family were to be secure under her watch.

She decided to widen the net of the rental's business by reaching out to further television companies and the many local theatres. Mimi had helped her a little once she was aware of the idea but she'd also been busy preparing for her move to Paris so Lottie knew there was a lot more mileage required behind her rentals' idea. She could ask Francine or Claude to check and correct her draft email and then she'd need to research how to reach the correct people. Perhaps Philippe might be interested to proof her draft but she'd not seen him since she left on Saturday morning even though they'd exchanged a couple of text messages.

Lottie was emotionally "at sea" as she missed Bob even though her world was so far removed from her life in

Marlow that she could have been on a different planet. She was unable to grasp why a fifty-six-year-old woman seemed to turn into a coy adolescent in Philippe's company. Was it the novelty of his French-ness or his adorable English accent when he occasionally expressed a whole sentence in English? Did she really like him when you stripped away the indisputable help he had given her? When she'd Skyped the kids, all of them had picked up on her mentioning his name and how he'd helped her at the police station, so they had started to ask about him on every call. At the best of times, they were continually worried for their mother, however, her involvement in some sort of drug running was a situation they'd never envisaged in the excitement of her owning a *brocante*. She was playing in shark-infested waters with professional drug dealers and Lottie had no idea her children were ringing each other on a regular basis to discuss whether their mother should come home. Even if they didn't know him, her children were relieved to hear her mention Philippe; this Frenchman who seemed to be supporting their mother physically and emotionally. Lottie found herself dismissing the friendship in a light-hearted fashion so they didn't exaggerate the relationship which she herself found confusing and complicated.

In an email exchange about photography and the light in the south of France, gym buddy Jill had asked if she'd found any good-looking models whilst she was out photographing the flora, fauna and the golden evening light that fell across the buildings. She'd found herself confiding in her about Philippe and her niggling doubts which resurfaced and put her on her guard. Jill was exhilarated at the idea of her best mate being hooked up with a Frenchman or at least being wined and dined by one of the natives. She understood her prudence but her friend deserved some happiness after the sudden loss of Bob and the discovery of another daughter. Jill was happily married so Lottie didn't know what to make of her comments that she would love to change places with her. This motivated Lottie to suggest a week's holiday or a long weekend so they could spend some girly time together and she could show her around the region without crowing or gloating about her transition from Marlow. She knew that there were people who envied her bravery and fearlessness. Celia at the Charity Shop had not replied to a couple of emails and Lottie could sense that this spirted woman was putting her own life under a microscope and making comparisons. Lottie did not know how to manage the predicament other than to be careful how she communicated her news from Avignon. She appreciated that an email might be received on a rainy day in Buckinghamshire so she downplayed certain news so that friends did not begrudge her metamorphosis from housewife to businesswoman in a region that seldom witnessed harsh weather. She felt she was losing touch with some people and it made her sad. She could understand losing contact with Robert's friends although she missed their endless golf chats in the sitting room after spending too long at the nineteenth hole. Had Frank and Smithie found a new playmate?

She loved receiving emails from Jill and had an inexplicable twinge of jealousy when gym buddy, Julia, declared she'd found a new friend to share the pain of the weekly workout. She had moments when she missed her house and her routines but there was no denying that, Brother Vialat apart, she was really very happy in Avignon and running the brocante. Lottie turned her mind back to the mailshot and began to play around with a few ideas.

The foot-soldiers through the shop in the morning were a mixed bunch. Some were buying and some were selling. It was not uncommon for people to walk in "on spec" clutching a valued treasure from their family home. Some might have a watch with a cracked face and a worn leather strap hanging off the lug end but others would have a beautiful beaded light which could be a bona fide Tiffany lamp or, at worst, a decent replica. They were equally as popular in France as at home which would have surprised the 19th century American, Louis Comfort Tiffany.

Lottie closed up at midday and wandered down to the shopping estate for a bite of lunch. She had a few favourite watering holes which were a brisk fifteen minutes' walk from work. Today, she decided to return to the department store, *Alinéa*, as they had a café/restaurant on the ground floor. She would never get used to a two-hour lunch and often walked back to the *brocante* and opened up at half past one. Nobody ever came in as mealtimes were sacrosanct and she'd quickly learnt business only interfered if you were participating in a lunch or dinner with work colleagues or clients. Since her arrival, she had witnessed the Mistral wind but there had been hardly any rain other than the day when it had fallen like stair-rods causing her to use her car to find a lunchtime tartine. The duration and intensity of the rainfall had amazed her so much that she had taken the sandwich and returned to the *brocante* to catch up on the accounts and paperwork.

Lottie appreciated the regular ebb and flow of her workload now that there was no more talk of books, drugs, Brother Vialat or the poor demised Brother Jean-Louis Pislait. She stayed in regular touch with Cédric as he'd become a dear friend and she knew he excitedly awaited news from "the outside world". She visited him every couple of weeks and would often find him in the garden now that the warm weather was a fixture. The retirement home had a beautiful garden. Some of the more able-bodied residents delighted in helping the gardening team who appeared once a month out of season and once a week when everything started to flower and flourish. There was a small vegetable plot that helped supplement the kitchen throughout the year and Madame Pillon and Monsieur Ravaux managed seedlings in a greenhouse just alongside the plot ensuring there was always something growing no matter the time of year. Lottie could see the change in Cédric now that he was no longer accountable for receiving shipments of books. He genuinely missed seeing the intricate work tooled in the leather and it was obvious that the odd repair of a belt or notepad for a resident didn't provide the same pleasure or satisfaction. Notwithstanding the sense of purpose that the deliveries gave him, he was worry-free and that, as Lottie recognised, was invaluable.

The two of them had no idea of any progress in the case of the cocaine shipments and the books. The matter had just vanished and the police were no longer in contact with either of them. They might have been rather surprised to learn of Brigadier-Chef Lepireon's plans if they'd known of the full-scale search being planned at *L'Abbaye de Notre Croix de Fer*. It took "worst case" and Capitaine Lebrun some days to arrange the search with the Commisariat in Lyon as they needed to outline the case, their evidence and request a layout of the building in advance so they could agree the best way that the Lyon team could be utilised. They didn't want to turn up understaffed or take more than a day to verify if the main building and any annexes had signs of drugs. They expected a verbal kicking from the Benedictine abbot who would not take kindly to a police team with dogs crawling over every inch of their monastic lives even though the search had to be alerted in advance given French law.

Lepireon and Lebrun drove the couple of hours up to the Commisariat in Lyon. Their counterparts had already delineated the roles of the twelve-member team which included two dog handlers. The Avignon crew addressed the members who were headed up by Capitaine Thierry Barreau. They explained the shipments of cocaine, the roles of Brother Jean-Louis Pislait and Brother Michel Vialat, the suspicious death of Brother Pislait and the shipment which surprisingly contained no drugs whatsoever. They ensured everyone knew their responsibilities and confirmed it would be an early raid starting at six o'clock. There were no "search warrants" as such in France even though applications were also made to the courts. The approval was given via a judge's letter of authority and the search could only be managed within defined hours of the day and with an owner's consent. Barreau had emailed the judge's letter to the abbot so he was forewarned of the invasion. The officers remained optimistic that Brother Vialat would be resident at the abbey and not away on business. They had a heightened interest in searching his quarters as they had no idea if the abbey was running an illicit drug operation or whether the corruption was restricted just to him or perhaps to several of the monks.

The morning of the raid arrived and the team gathered for one final briefing before agreeing a meeting point sited five minutes from the abbey. The cars gathered and drove in a tight convoy up to the abbey gates which were locked forcing them to ring the intercom and announce their arrival. The monk who responded didn't fully appreciate there was a whole team at the gate so he was completely taken aback when they all rolled up in a variety of police cars and vans; some marked and some unmarked. Fourteen police personnel were swarming in front of the abbey and an excited barking was coming from the rear of two of the vans. Capitaines Lebrun and Barreau requested to see the abbot and the anxious monk scurried off to relay that the abbey appeared to be under police siege. *"Aïe, la honte!"* he muttered under his breath as if the village would be pointing fingers at the brotherhood shouting "shame on you!"

The abbot arrived to greet his anticipated guests. His manner was composed and he appeared quite unruffled by the infiltration. He invited a senior member of the team to accompany him to his office and the detectives duly followed the abbot along a dark corridor to the interior of his private quarters. They explained they had reason to believe the abbey was arranging the movement and supply of narcotics and they had the original letter of authority from the judge endorsing their inspection of the premises and its outbuildings. The abbot didn't know whether to laugh or refute such a preposterous idea. He shook his head in bewilderment at such an absurd suggestion demanding to know what evidence they had to support such a ridiculous claim. Capitaine Serge Lebrun confirmed one of the brothers at the abbey was unquestionably involved and another brother, who might have been connected, had recently suffered an unfortunate and inexplicable death.

At this news the abbot challenged if they were talking about Brother Pislait. The two men confirmed they were indeed, and they witnessed a genuine sadness register on the face of the abbot. Brother Pislait had not been seen for several days and the last anyone knew of his movements seemed to confirm he was visiting his uncle; a trip he made regularly to ensure the old man was well and looking after himself. was not unusual for him to stay overnight but he had not returned to the abbey and his fellow brothers were worried by his continued absence. The two policemen requested authority to allow the officers and the dog handlers to access the rooms in the abbey which was duly granted on the proviso they did not enter the Prayer Room which was for silent contemplation. The senior officers agreed that they would not enter it until the very end of the search but that every part of the building was included in their search warrant. The abbot was about to complain but his mind was still trying to absorb a possible narcotics operation and he found himself acknowledging the warrant and acquiescing to their full search. Capitaine Barreau explained that they required everyone in the abbey to be fingerprinted and there would be no exceptions. One of the team would be dedicated to this activity and all monks and any civilian staff would need to be identified and registered. The abbot accepted this was a necessary detail of the search.

Given both of the policemen were unclear of the abbot's involvement, they guardedly asked the whereabouts of Brother Michel Vialat. For the first time since their arrival, the abbot's face visibly blanched at the mention of another member of his team apart from Jean-Louis. He explained that Brother Michel was the abbey's sacrist and, therefore, responsible for the abbey's items of value. The senior officers asked him to elaborate and he explained that the abbey had a number of ecclesiastical treasures and the sacrist ensured their safe movement to other abbeys which were open to the public. L'Abbaye de Notre Croix de Fer did not open to the public and had not done so for over fifty years. Brother Michel was a solid and dependable person who the abbot respected and hoped would replace him when the good Lord decided his days on earth were over. The detective team acknowledged the importance of the role and asked if Brother Michel could be brought to them. They did not wish to discuss their reasons why he was required so the abbot was forced to step out of his quarters and ask one of the monks to bring Brother Michel to his office.

The Avignon detective met Brother Michel Vialat in person for the first time. He had viewed the security camera image provided by Madame Pearce and seen the Evidence Board photos and so was not surprised by the man's appearance. He was, however, much taller than he had expected and there was something about his stance as he assuredly walked into the office. He had a steely cold composure and expressed neither surprise nor disinterest at the policemen's demand to search his room. The abbot apologised to Brother Michel for the disruption, however, the purpose of the search was important to their enquiries and the abbot had consented to the inspection of the abbey and its outbuildings. Brother Michel and the abbot were the first people to have their fingerprints taken and they shared a supportive glance as they wiped the ink from their hands. "Venez avec moi, s'il vous plaît. Ma chambre personnelle est au premier étage" Brother Michel declared as he strolled out of the abbot's office and headed towards the staircase with the two men a few steps behind him. Although he added his own questions regarding their visit both men inwardly noted his demeanour as if this was an everyday occurrence.

They took one of the dogs up to search Vialat's room on the first floor and it was obvious that the dog was reacting to narcotic traces but there was no sign of anything suspicious as the man remained quietly in the corner of the room with a bemused look on his face. The team searched, prodded and probed until four o'clock without a hint of anything untoward. The outbuildings underwent a thorough investigation and the dogs were becoming tired and the detectives were frustrated by the lack of any substantial evidence. One of the dog handlers was on the lawn just in front of the abbey and alongside their cars. Sia, an elderly labrador retriever, was enjoying a light rough and tumble to re-stimulate her as she was one of the older dogs in the corps. She was one week away from a well-earned retirement and she found she just didn't have the stamina any more when there was nothing to find and nobody gave her the ball that she almost loved more than food itself. She was a very particular dog with an independent streak that set her apart from her chums back at headquarters. She had a number of stories she could recount following her many years with Florian as they made an excellent team. They had a number of medals to their name; not least the one for bravery. Florian had been under attack in a warehouse and Sia knew he was in difficulty when he was confronted by three men who were not running away. One of the men came at Florian with a knife and Sia knew that this must not happen as she loved Florian as if he was her pack leader. She charged at the man and took a knife into her chest that caused her to stop in her tracks looking up at her buddy in shock and pain whilst pleading for him to be safe.

What followed was months of recuperation for both Sia and for Florian who lost a kilo in the two weeks when it remained touch and go if Sia would pull through. This was the level of devotion between them even though Florian had worked with other dogs in the past. A dog's life in the police force would only be for a few years but it was inevitable that they became interwoven as each relied upon the other. No dog had touched Florian as much as Sia and now he knew she'd spent a long day finding nothing and he'd taken her for a few minutes' distraction out in the fresh air. He dreaded next week arriving even though Bruno was waiting in the wings as a newly fledged beagle who seemed to be a very promising replacement. Dog handlers were a different breed and his mates at the station never asked after him without asking after Sia. They went together and when you talked about one then you needed to talk about the other. Florian was just about to bring her back in to carry on the search of the remaining rooms when Sia went charging off across the lawn towards a small thicket.

Florian called after her angrily as she sometimes had a habit of picking up the scent of a rabbit or a wild boar and it never ended positively as Florian could spend ten minutes trying to get her back. He set off to follow her muttering under his breath that it was just one more week and for God's sake just cut him some slack. He pushed through the dense bushes and swore as branches hit him in the face or he trod unevenly on a rock causing him to lose balance. "*Sia, retournez tout de suite*" he shouted in the hope she really would come back to him. He could hear her ahead of him and she was barking excitedly. Had she found someone? He pushed on through the trees and then, all of a sudden, he was in a clearing and in front of him was a stone building. Clearly it was in-keeping with the abbey as it had the signs of being built in the 17th century and it had also been restored and was in good condition.

Sia was in front of a wooden door jumping up and down and barking excitedly. Florian felt confident that she couldn't detect anything at that distance and tried to encourage her to return to the abbey with him; after all they had another hour or so before they would finish the search.

Sia sat down and looked at him defiantly. Florian knew that look only too well. Sia was telling him this was important and needed further investigation. He tried the door but it was locked so they would need to go and get the key. He didn't know if the other dog handler had already searched this building as Florian had been given a number of rooms in the abbey. Sia trotted alongside him accepting that the door didn't open so her mate must be going for something to make it open and then she could have a good look inside as she hated closed doors when she had a job to do.

Florian reported back to his superior about the building hidden among the bushes and trees which he felt certain was not on the plans they'd been shown back in the office. Florian and his superior returned to the abbot's office with Sia devotedly trotting behind. The abbot explained the building was a mausoleum and columbaria. Previous abbots were interred inside the mausoleum, or their remains were in sceptred, decorated urns. The monks rarely entered the building and the only person who entered did so every two months as he trusted one of the almoners to ensure everything was tidy, the roof was still intact and there were no obvious maintenance issues. Brother Anton and his key were requisitioned to meet the dog handler and his senior officer at the mausoleum immediately as they both set off again to await his arrival. The senior officer pressed the button down on his walkie-talkie to instruct Capitaine Barreau that there was an additional building which was not recorded on the plan.

Brother Anton scurried into the small copse with an enormous key hanging from a wooden block. There were three wards at the base of the key that manipulated the lock and the size of the stem was far from your conventional key width. It was finished off with a decorated metal plate at the

114

end depicting a monk which Brother Anton explained was
Le Père d'Abbé Christian, the founder of the abbey. The
men stood back as he opened up the mausoleum and
allowed the monk to enter first. Sia momentarily respected
the monk accessing the building but then she shot in as
there was a job to be done. She explored the nooks and
crannies of the stone building. The smell of the interior
certainly confirmed that this was not a building regularly
exposed to fresh air and she was momentarily distracted by
the odour of rodents but Florian whispered instructions to
her and she got herself back on track. They were pretty
much coming to the conclusion that this was just another
building that had somehow been omitted from the plans
when Sia sat bolt upright alongside one of the stone
sarcophagi. This told Florian that there was yet again
something of interest and that she'd detected drugs or
something that was on the banned list following her
intensive training. The two men set about trying to slide the
lid of the sarcophagus to one side causing Brother Anton to
spin around in horror and scream at them to stop. He was
almost sobbing as he explained the tomb was sacrosanct
and it was totally forbidden to expose the remains of
deceased abbots. They must see the living abbot if they
wanted to open the sarcophagus of *Le Père d'Abbé
Christian* who was to be respected no matter how important
their search might be.

Once more, the two men and Sia returned to the main
building to gain the abbot's permission. He reaffirmed that
opening the sarcophagus was indeed forbidden and, seeing
their rigid expressions, also asked that they respect the
abbey and its predecessors. He had accommodated them
all day and now he needed some leniency regarding his
forebears. The men retreated to seek out the advice of

Capitaine Barreau who decided to accompany them to the mausoleum and see the dog's reaction.

None of them could dispute that Sia was showing every sign that the sarcophagus was of interest to her and, therefore, to them. The Lyon detective said he would return to the abbot and request that the lid be partially removed to permit a closer inspection. The abbot was understandably sickened at the news and said he would accompany them to the building to ensure they respected the founder's resting place. He crossed the lawns of the abbey with his head bowed and the worries of the world on his shoulders. He was no longer the unruffled and quietly spoken man whom they had met on arrival. The policemen sensed he was trying hard to contain an anger that was quelling in his body.

He sprinkled Holy Water over the tomb as the detective and Florian used their combined strength to slide the stone lid partially towards the wall. They tried not to look at the crumbling remains of the abbot or the traces of his robes that had long disintegrated. By now Sia was clawing up at the sarcophagus which just added to the abbot's pleas of respect. They were on the verge of closing back the lid when the detective declared "*attendez*" and he put on yet another pair of blue latex gloves and delved into the stone cavity. From the stone burial chamber, he withdrew a plastic bag of beige powder. The abbot was now beside himself muttering and lamenting the invasion as if the remains of the deceased abbot could somehow hear him. He fell quiet when the beige powder was extricated and looked awkward and shocked at the illicit item sharing *Père Christian's* resting place. Given it was clear this was an alien item, he permitted the lid to be moved to allow visibility to the rest of the tomb. Thierry Barreau went outside to get a twig and returned to delicately push aside the faded robes. The action exposed at least eight more bags of drugs sharing the same space as the 17th century *père*. Sia sat down having finished her work and Florian took her outside to play ball in acknowledgement of her sterling work – yet again!

Barreau went back to the abbey with the abbot and the almoner having left Florian keeping guard over the drugs. He found Capitaine Lebrun and Brigadier-Chef Lepireon and requested they follow him back to the mausoleum explaining on route that one of the dogs had located a number of bags of powder. They entered the stone building and couldn't disguise their surprise at the hiding place of the bags. Lepireon had her test kit and it was just a matter of seconds before they had the confirmation they needed that the contents were indeed narcotics and more precisely cocaine. They had found nothing in Brother Michel Vialat's room other than watching the dog react to what was probably some residual traces. Now they understood as maybe the drugs had been moved to this building and to a beloved tomb which nobody was permitted to touch. They bagged up the drugs and placed them in one of the evidence trunks in the car which was duly locked and alarmed.

They returned inside the main building where they finished meticulously and painstakingly searching the remaining rooms looking for further evidence or some proof which might indicate who or how many monks were involved. The monks silently retreated to other areas of the abbey when the team ended their search in the Prayer Room. Many of them had found the search to be an invasion of their privacy and of their minds and there were a number who expressed their disapproval to the abbot who they held responsible for permitting the inspection. The senior monk decided not to disclose the search findings to his fellow brothers as he was impatient to return the abbey to a sanctuary of calm and order. What could be gained by them knowing there had been a discovery of drugs? He felt ashamed and upset that someone in his brotherhood was responsible and he thought it highly unlikely it was Brother Anton or Brother Michel. He instructed the almoner to refrain from sharing any information and to bring him the key to the mausoleum which would now be his sole responsibility. As the final car swept out the abbey's driveway, the troubled abbot returned to his study to consider what had just occurred and who was responsible.

CHAPTER SEVEN
THE CORNER PIECES

Once the team returned to the police station in Lyon, everyone de-briefed and the evidence box went for fingerprint analysis to verify if the plastic sleeves of cocaine contained any fingerprint traces. Capitaine Lebrun and Brigadier-Chef Lepireon realised they now had a crime covering two regions as Lyon was in the Rhône department and located in the Auvergne-Rhône-Alpes region whilst Avignon was in the Vaucluse department in the Provence-Alpes-Côte d'Azur region. It would, undoubtedly, create some difficulties but there was important evidence in both locations. One had been the source of identifying the drugs together with a death which they now agreed was murder. The host team, under the authority of Thierry Barreau, was at the root of the drug supply, however, they still did not know how many people were involved in the narcotics shipments or the end destination of the cocaine.

They could count the search a success but their findings only raised many more unanswered questions. The Avignon team had an overnight authorised in the station budget as it was accepted that neither of the officers should complete a two hour return journey to Avignon after a full day's search. Lebrun and Lepireon agreed to meet back at the Lyon station in the morning to determine their next course of action with Barreau. They would have liked to sample the delights that the city had to offer but the reality was two extremely knackered officers who only dreamt of a quick meal and their beds. They were both delighted that the drugs had been located towards the end of the day as it had looked increasingly unlikely that anything would be found in any of the rooms at the abbey. They agreed that Brother Michel Vialat was a "cool" character with a somewhat brazen manner goading them to find evidence against him. Thank heavens for Sia and Florian as the mausoleum was well concealed; be that deliberate or out of respect for the sleeping occupants. They swapped theories on the drive back to the hotel, grabbed a mediocre dinner, and passed out having consumed one or two miniatures from their respective mini bars.

The next morning, the team meeting took less than an hour as Barreau and a handful of officers agreed to concentrate on the movement of historical artefacts together with their responsibility for the fingerprint analysis. The Avignon team advised they would investigate the relationship between Brother Pislait and Brother Vialat in the hope of finding some link.   They would determine the next course of action once they knew more from their combined investigations.

Capitaine Lebrun needed to stay in Avignon once they had returned to the city. He needed to work with Lepireon and have access to Monsieur Mallet and perhaps to Madame Pearce. The Brigadier-Chef was driving the motorway route back to the South so he was free to contact his department head in OCRTIS (*Office Central pour la Répression du Trafic Illicite des Stupéfiants*) as he would need to request an extension to his secondment. He briefed him on the search at the abbey in Lyon and the finding of the additional packets of drugs confirmed as cocaine. He detailed the next phase of the investigation and was delighted to receive confirmation of a week's extension which would be reviewed once there was a further update. He would have preferred his apartment in Marseille to the *Police Municipale* apartment but at least it wasn't a sterile hotel. Given Avignon attracted a huge number of tourists in the summer, the *Municipale* rented the apartment for the overflow of additional officers who descended from the north to help police during the summer season.

They arrived back at the station, returned all the files and data to the cupboards and updated the Evidence Board. One of the brigadiers was keen to inform them of an update on the CCTV data. Lepireon knew the initial search of the cameras in the main street had brought forth nothing of interest. Yes, they could identify Madame Pearce, Brother Pislait and behind him Brother Vialat. They had footage of the accident but nothing could be construed from the findings or any blame attributed. She'd been aware of this before the trip to Lyon but she also knew that two officers were working on footage acquired from the shops. Many of them had CCTV footage capturing people coming in and going out of their premises. The latter was useful for shoplifting cases as the footage proved the culprits had definitely exited the shop without paying. The Brigadier invited Capitaine Lebrun and his superior, Lepireon, to take a seat and he would show them both his discovery.

Force of habit drove the Brigadier-Chef to check the date and time of the tape to ensure it corresponded with the timeframe reported by Madame Pearce. She noted the name of the shop that had provided the tape and sat back to view the footage. *"J'en ai plusieurs films parce que chacun est important"* explained the junior member of staff as he wanted to show an earlier tape from one of the other stores to verify the timeframe. He grabbed a pencil to point out Madame Pearce hastening up the road towards the *Place de l'Horloge* with the tape clearly showing Brother Pislait shouting something to her and her lack of reaction. There was no sign of Brother Vialat in the picture but then he loaded another tape onto the machine. Once more you had the ability to see Madame Pearce rush past the frontage of the shop followed by Brother Pislait but now Brother Vialat was right behind his colleague. What followed shocked them all as Brother Vialat spun Pislait around, kneed him at the back of his legs so they gave way and he pushed him almost horizontally under the wheels of the speeding lorry.

It was over in seconds and they watched as fellow shoppers gathered to try and verify exactly what had just happened. The truck driver could be seen exiting his cab and all but collapsing at the sight of the man under his wheels. Vialat was nowhere to be seen and the Brigadier asked them to wait whilst he loaded the last of the tapes. In this one you could see the monk hurrying down the road and into McDonalds. Some minutes later, Vialat exited with his cuculla under his arm appearing identical to the other shoppers in a shirt and beige jeans. He looked just like another member of the public even though he'd just murdered a man.

The senior officers congratulated the junior brigadier on his evidence which could prove Brother Vialat had killed Jean-Louis Pislait. Now they needed to understand why someone in the brotherhood had chosen to kill a fellow monk. What was the link between the two ecclesiastical brothers apart from their roles at the abbey? It was clear that Brother Vialat was worried what might happen if his colleague caught up with Madame Pearce and he'd taken desperate measures to prevent it from happening. It was also clear that he wanted to avoid any form of contact between the two people. They'd already run checks against Jean-Louis Pislait and knew of his criminal past and difficulties with petty theft up until he seemed to join the abbey when any negative records came to an abrupt halt. They had only made a cursory check on Brother Vialat because of his threats to Madame Pearce and his possible criminal action regarding her car. They decided to delve deeper to try and find a link between the two men as both were monks but what was the common link between them? Lepireon and Lebrun sat across from each other as they accessed the records on the two computers. The clock ticked away the minutes until Lepireon uttered *"intéressant"* as she toggled between screens covering crimes and screens that noted prison terms. Lebrun looked up at her quizzically as he continued his own foray through the endless database until she abruptly declared *"voilà, trouvé"*. Lebrun asked what she'd found as Lepireon confirmed that both men had been in prison at the same time. Jean-Louis had served five years for the death of his father whilst Michel Vialat had been in the same prison for supplying narcotics; there was no reference to the abbey or their role as monks prior to Pislait's or Vialat's prison term.

Capitaine Serge Lebrun rang the gaol and requested more data on the two of them. He appreciated the records might not be easily accessible after all this time. They took his contact details and promised to get back to him as quickly as possible. As the day came to a close, they had another piece of the puzzle in place as the prison confirmed they had shared a cell until Michel Vialat was released early on parole.

The Avignon team now had enough to prove Brother Michel Vialat was responsible for his colleague's death and they could prove a connection between the two of them. They could also prove that Brother Vialat had taken over responsibility of collecting the consignments from his cellmate's uncle. Now they needed to know what the Lyon team had discovered as there had been no news from their end during the day.

Lyon were delighted with their colleagues' progress and Capitaine Barreau confirmed that they were ploughing through the paperwork regarding the loan of artefacts to museums and private collectors. They were paying particular attention to any invoices for the sale of ecclesiastical textbooks and one gallery was flagged up for further investigation. Their Southern friends announced they needed to return and interview Brother Vialat and would be prepared to show him the tapes to demonstrate that he had killed Jean-Louis Pislait. They agreed to drive up the next day and requested the commissariat pick him up around late morning and bring him in for questioning. They bagged up their findings, ensured copies were taken of some of the documents, and headed off for a quiet night before a very early start.

The next morning, the officers shared the motorway driving and the mood between them relaxed as they dipped into personal topics of conversation as well as the case. The latter was first and foremost on their minds but the hours they'd now spent together had shifted the dynamic and they felt more comfortable to talk of family and their careers. Both were quite surprised, if not anxious, to receive a call from Barreau just an hour into their journey as there was still a good hour to go before arriving at the hospital even though the motorway was running freely. Serge Lebrun put his mobile on speaker phone and they both exchanged looks as they heard Brother Michel Vialat was in the *Hôpital de Die* where he was undergoing surgery for a bullet to his shoulder. Capitaine Barreau was on route to interview him, once he was capable of speaking, so was suggesting they meet at the hospital rather than go to the station. They both agreed that it made sense to divert to the new location and asked if there were any other known facts but nothing more was forthcoming.

They pulled into the hospital car park and called their colleague who came down to meet them in Reception. The monk was out of surgery and was now in a recovery room with a brigadier stationed outside to ensure his safety. The doctors had suggested another hour before he would be strong enough to support questioning, therefore, they headed off to the cafeteria for a snack and a coffee and to agree interview tactics. Although they had the tapes to hand, they'd had the foresight to take screen images of the key moments that proved Vialat's murder of his friend. They would be needed now that the questioning would not be at the station. They showed their colleague the evidence and agreed Lebrun would drive the session. Once the refreshments had been consumed, they headed towards the lift as there were only ten minutes remaining of the doctor's recommended timeline. The Brigadier stood to attention as they approached and confirmed that there had been no activity. They strode into the private room to find a much-diminished character to the cool, assertive Brother Vialat they'd met at the abbey. He was awake and eyed them suspiciously albeit recognising that he now had police protection. Everyone pulled up a chair and they asked him to explain how he'd been shot.

He confirmed he was on his way to the courier's depot as the abbey had agreed to provide a triptych, two chalices and three bronze plates to an exhibition being held at an abbey near Fleury. Everything was wrapped up and contained in three boxes and the smallest one was alongside him on the passenger's seat. The only thing he could remember was breaking suddenly to avoid a muntjac deer and the parcel slipping off the seat. He'd lent over to secure the box and, at the same time, he heard the rear window smash and sensed a car speed past him. He'd lost control of the vehicle and smashed through the sapling trees until he hit a large one which brought him to a complete stop. In the first few seconds, he thought he was uninjured except for a head wound but then he realised he had a screaming pain from his shoulder and assumed it was all part of the accident. It was only when a car travelling the same road stopped to investigate his crashed vehicle that they discovered he was bleeding from his head and also from his shoulder. The couple had phoned for an ambulance and, while they waited, the driver confirmed there was a hole in his rear seat and it appeared to be aligned to his shoulder and the blood coming from his robe. Brother Vialat remembered arriving at the hospital having insisted the ambulance personnel take his valuable boxes. As he lay on the gurney, he heard someone confirm his facial injuries and that a bullet had entered the rear of his left shoulder and he'd need surgery. He had no idea who had shot him or why.

As they talked to him, they heard a knock at the door and the abbot entered. He was surprised and concerned to see the group surrounding his fellow brother given he'd only just been released from surgery. He had come to collect the parcels which had been in the car in order they remained secure and under the control of the abbey. They were extremely important relics from the 16th century and the abbot had no idea of their current value. The combination of the abbot and his desire to retrieve the parcels caused the three police officers to insist each parcel was opened. All of the items could be easily checked other than the wooden frames surrounding the triptych. They decided that the items were drug free and their destination might not be a judicious location for distributing narcotics. They allowed the abbot to remove the items and halted the interview whilst he made the couple of trips to his car.

They returned to questioning Brother Vialat and Capitaine Lebrun changed the tone of the interview by announcing he was under arrest for the murder of his prison cellmate, Brother Jean-Louis Pislait. Brother Vialat shrank back in the bed protesting his innocence whilst digesting the fact they knew he'd been in the same prison and even the same cell. They had him on the "back foot" and they knew it. They opened the files to share their evidence wondering what reasons he could provide to vindicate himself from pushing his friend under the truck. Michel Vialat looked at the series of photos and began to cry. The change in emotion did little to divert the group's mission and they ploughed on insisting on why he had murdered his friend.

Brother Vialat's head was spinning from the moment he'd come round from the operation. His life was over unless he could create a new life and he confirmed to the officers that he was now extremely frightened for his own safety. The people who had instructed him to kill his friend were still out there and he felt sure they would make a further attempt to kill him. The abbey was not an easy place to hide from his potential assassins and he insisted that he would only disclose what he knew if he had police protection which could ultimately mean a total change to the way he lived his life. None of them acknowledged the police protection although Barreau noted guardedly that the request depended upon what he would tell them. Vialat knew the explanation would take some time and shifted uneasily in his bed as he began his story.

He explained about his early drug involvement and moving into distribution. He found himself in prison where he appreciated the friendship that grew with Jean-Louis. Vialat had been released earlier than his friend but they remained in touch. They'd both experienced enormous difficulty in finding work as nobody could see further than their prison record. Nearly a year later, Vialat was approached by a man who had somehow found out about his drug history. He explained that he was part of a community which they chose to call "The Sarabaites" who were infiltrating abbeys to either steal relics or create and develop criminal activities. Lepireon had heard of sarabaite monks but they were still men of god so this other faction were clearly on a completely different mission. Brother Vialat said they made the life, albeit monastic, sound rewarding for him personally and by then his pecuniary existence and knock backs from job interviews were taking their toll. It wasn't a difficult decision as he preferred to sacrifice his mundane, struggling life for one that might create a degree of comfort in a few years' time. He had listened to the potential benefits, the money he could make, and underwent a month of training so he would not do or say anything within his appointed abbey that might cause the abbot or fellow monks to question his faith or character. He'd been with *L'Abbaye de Notre Croix de Fer* for a number of years and he'd been very happy. He covered his head in his hands and began to cry once more. The police officers waited for him to compose himself.

Brother Vialat said he had recruited Jean-Louis as he was also unable to find a job and consequently was homeless and living on scraps. He also had no purpose or any comforts in his life so he'd invited his friend to be part of his own new world even though there were risks involved and it was fabricated on lies and criminal activity. Vialat confirmed Jean-Louis had not jumped at the idea of a roof over his head or a hot meal as he was fundamentally a good man who knew it involved illegal acts against the abbey. He had no desire to return to prison which he had found both mentally and physically challenging. It was many months later that he'd approached Michel to ask him to explain about the training in more detail. Even during the fast-track initiation into monastic life, it was clear that Jean-Louis was not convinced that he was doing the right thing as he remained conflicted and troubled throughout the tuition period. This lack of commitment had been noted by the trainers resulting in Jean-Louis joining his friend at the abbey in Lyon where Michel had already been involved in some minor drug crimes.

With Jean-Louis on board, whoever was masterminding the "bigger plan" conceived a new route for the acquisition of drugs. He has no idea how they knew of Monsieur Mallet or his skill in leather working. They set up a plan of deliveries of tooled leather books which would be sold to museums, galleries and some private collectors. After all, the old man's domestic address, together with his talent and former business in leather, would be the perfect foil to any enquiring eyes. At the beginning, the deliveries were clean of drugs as they tested the system and then they altered the deliveries so that one in two contained drugs in the spines and these were routed by the two of them to a specific address. The "safe" books were imported in higher quantities so that there were always clean orders going to a number of different destinations which avoided authorities questioning the imported consignments and reduced the possibility that any narcotics tests would prove positive.

The books tended to come from locations in South America but there were also supplies from the East African coast and the Middle East.

Jean-Louis was happy to rekindle his friendship with Michel and they were both relieved to have a roof over their heads and share the companionship of their fellow monks. Yes, they missed women and all they had to offer but they'd both known homelessness and austerity and the abbey was an easy adjustment for the two men. Everything was working well even though they were cuckoos in the nest of the Benedictine monks. Michel had even been promoted over a few years to the cherished position of sacrist and they remained content, even elated, until the day Jean-Louis' uncle sold the books to the British woman. Michel Vialat could never have imagined the direction their lives would take after such an innocent decision by Monsieur Mallet. The timing had been disastrous and he knew Jean-Louis berated himself for not collecting the books before they could be sold to her. They both knew the consignment contained cocaine and that they had to get the four books back in their custody before anyone could discover the narcotics and blow the operation wide open.

In the beginning Michel had not had any involvement other than supporting his cellmate friend through his anxieties. He knew Jean-Louis was under pressure as the consignment had not been shipped to the people expecting the drugs. Capitaine Barreau stopped to affirm "La Galerie d'Art et des Artefacts"? Michel Vialat nodded realising they already knew of its existence. He continued that he'd received a phone call regarding Jean-Louis as the distributors were questioning his allegiance to their operation and why they were still waiting for their shipment. They asked him to investigate and report back immediately.

Jean-Louis was an emotional mess as he didn't want his uncle aware of his nephew's further fall from grace or for his relative to be in danger. His uncle's help providing a realistic cost on the books had been appreciated by everyone up to the point he unwittingly sold a shipment without approval. The British woman was an innocent pawn in their crimes and Jean-Louis was finding it harder and harder to live with himself as he continuously berated his weak nature given he'd always been a good man and known right from wrong. The world's lack of trust in providing him a decent job and a home after prison had pushed him down a route that had been acceptable for a couple of years until it was now starting to unravel. Michel and Jean-Louis had discussed several times how to resolve the matter but Michel knew that Jean-Louis' conscience was pushing him to explain everything to Madame Pearce and to get the books back to his safe custody. The morning of the accident, Michel had been instructed to follow Jean-Louis and he had been on the phone to the gallery to explain Jean-Louis was clearly trying to talk to Madame Pearce and he had some idea of the subject matter. This was when he was instructed to stop him at all costs. The individual on the phone gave him an ultimatum and should he fail, he would find himself beheaded and dismembered with the pieces of his body dropped into weighted sacks and thrown into the *Rhône*.

Michel Vialat already knew of the demise of two of the recruits who had stepped out of turn and he did not doubt the sincerity of their claim. He had shouted to Jean-Louis to stop pursuing the woman and to please speak to him but he refused to accept his friend's help. Vialat repeated three or four times that he had no choice as his friend would not stop pursuing Madame Pearce. He could not eradicate the horror in his friend's eyes as he'd pushed him into the road; the mixture of hurt and despair in those eyes never left him. "Pas de choix, je n'avais pas de choix" he repeated until the monitors alongside him started beeping and buzzing which brought a nurse hurrying into the room. She checked on her patient and advised a doctor would need to verify his condition. She suggested the officers were exhausting her patient and she thought they ought to leave. None of the officials were about to obey until a doctor put paid to the interview by insisting they all leave immediately.

The team spoke briefly with the Brigadier outside the room and confirmed that they would arrange for a shift system to be put in place. Brother Michel Vialat was under arrest and was also at risk of a further threat on his own life. The Brigadier was to remain vigilant and always remain outside the patient's room until the shift system was operational. The police officer acknowledged the instructions.

They drove in convoy back to station where Capitaine Thierry Barreau set up the hospital rota to secure the safety of Brother Vialat. They moved to the Evidence Board which was a duplicate of the one in Avignon. They started to update it following the information gleaned from the patient.

CHAPTER EIGHT
THE DATING GAME

Lottie was relishing her new life managing the *brocante*. She had easily settled into Mimi's apartment which she found comfortable and welcoming after a long day at Le Pontet. She regularly took an evening glass of wine out to the garden and had even met one or two of the other residents over the warm summer months. To her, it would always be Mimi's apartment so it was only natural she regularly questioned whether she should buy a property of her own or whether it was too soon given her metamorphosis was still in its infancy.

She had followed through the idea to contact the television and theatre companies via email which Francine and Claude had checked for errors and syntax. The three of them had created a contact list of broadcasting and playhouse institutions and then split out the responsibility of finding email addresses for the designers and prop buyers. Lottie was working on her section of the list when she picked up a call from Philippe. In the last few days, they'd exchanged text messages theorising what might be happening at the *Police Municipale* office and considering any progress they might have made in the case. Philippe had also been in and out of the *brocante* either collecting repairs or returning furniture items and he always came up to the office to share a coffee with her and chat about nothing in particular. She found herself loving their little chats or hearing her phone ping an alert of a text message with his name visible on the screen. The children were still exploring what sort of relationship she had with him. Thomas and Alison's questioning was subtle and indirect but this was not the case with Elouise who demanded to know the details and if she'd discovered if he wore Y-fronts yet. Lottie was shocked, berating her and suggesting her dad would be horrified. This just caused Lou to remind her she was still a relatively young woman at fifty-six and weren't there any decent Frenchmen to be found anywhere in Avignon?

She picked up Philippe's call and found it was an invitation to dinner with him and his daughter Natalie. Her mind automatically returned to the dinner at his house the day her tyres had been destroyed. Without question, she really liked him but she still worried whether she trusted him. There had been his embarrassed and clumsy rejection of a phone call when she'd entered the kitchen and the clumsy kiss – what was that all about? Perhaps she'd find out more if she accepted the invitation, so she went ahead and said "yes, when?" One week later Lottie was to reflect how this decision was the catalyst of change in their relationship.

Lottie wasn't too sure on the etiquette of going to a French home for an evening meal. What did you take a man and his daughter? She opted for a high-end bottle of red wine and some flowers. She had no idea if he was a "flower" man but she decided Natalie could always take them home if they weren't a conventional choice. She selected one of the few dresses from her wardrobe and accompanied the simple navy shift dress with a small red bolero jacket. She lived in jeans and casual trousers at the emporium as they were comfortable and practical; an absolute necessity as she moved items around the rooms to tempt buyers to part with their cash. She added her silver earrings and a dab of Issey Miyake and analysed herself in the mirror. She approved of her make-up and even the risqué bright red lipstick. Her hair seemed to react better to blow-drying with the harsh water and the soft waves didn't seem to need any artificial fixer so she returned the hairspray to the bathroom. She peered into the mirror above the washbasin "not too shabby Lottie love" she mused accepting the crow's feet at the corner of her eyes. She pimped and preened wondering what was going on with the area between her nose and her top lip as grooves were forming that had not been there five years ago. "Go Girl!" chuckled Lottie as she switched off Charlie Parker who had provided the musical accompaniment whilst she was dressing.

She drew up outside Philippe's house feeling a little jittery and skittish at the thought of the evening ahead even though his daughter would be present. She took a deep breath and imagined a slurp from a glass of wine which she felt sure would steady the anxiety of accepting her first "date" since losing Bob. It was a huge relief that Natalie was at the dinner as it removed the previous intimacy of two people sharing a meal. She'd parked alongside the house, switched off the engine and checked her lipstick once more in the mirror. Clutching the bottle and the flowers, she rang the doorbell and heard Philippe's cheery "*J'arrive*" as he made his way to the front door.

The customary three kisses were exchanged and he escorted her into the kitchen where Natalie was washing some green haricot beans. She turned off the tap and turned to meet her. She coyly extended her hand expressing "*Enchantée, Madame Pearce*" but Lottie opted to put down the flowers and bottle and give her three kisses as a natural and obvious choice of greeting. "*Mais non, c'est Lottie ou Charlotte"* she declared causing Natalie to exchange an appreciative look with her father at the lack of formality. Philippe was thanking Lottie for the wine which he confirmed they would drink with the meal. For now, she was being offered a glass of rosé or a glass of white wine; Lottie opted for rosé. She explained that Philippe might like fresh flowers in the house but, if not, she was sure Natalie would enjoy them. He laughed at her suggestion and confirmed that he loved flowers and there was no way his daughter would be having them. Natalie feigned disappointment as Philippe enquired whether Lottie would like to remove her jacket.

Natalie was a pretty woman who Lottie estimated to be around twenty-five. She had long blond hair like Alison and Lottie thought of her daughter as the blue eyes darted up and down taking in her father's friend. Lottie declared the smells in the kitchen were wonderful and Natalie explained they would be eating a *gigot d'agneau* with dauphinoise potatoes and green beans. Lottie was glad she'd brought a bottle of red wine as it would work well with the roast lamb and she turned to accept the glass of rosé that was being offered to her.

They all moved to the sitting room where they relaxed with a selection of olives and potato chips and Natalie responded to an amiable probing by Lottie. She remembered Philippe advising she was a secretary for a pool of surgeons at a hospital in Avignon but she didn't know much more about her. Natalie confirmed she was engaged to a young lad called Mo Fahkri who her father found "acceptable" for his only daughter. Lottie's further questions identified that Natalie and Mo were working hard to afford a house and they were still deciding if they wanted to marry or just live together. Philippe's eyes went to the ceiling as Natalie confirmed marriage was not a certainty causing Lottie to explain that her eldest daughter hadn't married but was now in a good relationship which she also hoped would end in a marriage proposal although they seemed dead against it.

Philippe realised he needed to check on the gigot and potatoes. The table was already laid so he suggested they find a seat and start the entrée. Natalie brought out the foie gras and salad and returned to the kitchen to collect the fig chutney and a basket of melba toast. The trio all talked easily and openly about a wide variety of subjects. Natalie had a sensible head on her shoulders and didn't seem to have been affected by her parents' split. Lottie didn't know how long ago Philippe had separated from his wife but Natalie soon chipped in that their divorce had been nine years ago. Once the entrée had been consumed, the chef returned to the kitchen to cook the French beans. The noise of saucepans being shifted and the oven door opening caused both women to pick up their glasses and walk through to join him.

He took the lamb out to let it settle and put a heat under the beans which he part boiled and then flash panned with garlic and butter. Philippe started to make a jus from the shallots that had been under the joint adding a selection of herbs and red wine and a small amount of flour. He boiled a kettle to add a little vegetable stock. Lottie admired the orchestrated and confident way he moved around the kitchen; he was clearly in his element and a natural chef. She popped back into the dining room to gather up the dishes and left them on a centre unit. Natalie took charge of the jus as Philippe opened the bottle of red wine and she hoped it was as good as its price and the shop owner's glowing description. Within a few minutes they were back at the table and conversation returned to the *brocante* and then onto Lottie's awful experience relating to the books. She confirmed that Philippe's assistance had been invaluable both at the police station and as a comfort during such an awful period. Natalie asked the current status of the investigations and Lottie confirmed that she no idea.

The conversation ebbed and flowed in a cheerful exchange where one minute Lottie was recounting bits of her life in Britain, Philippe was talking of tricky restorations and Natalie was bemoaning why men could be so difficult to understand. The wine flowed and Lottie was delighted that Philippe and Natalie both remarked on the quality of her gift. She refused a white wine with her dessert which was a luscious home-baked cherry *clafoutis* accompanied with a slightly tart *crème fraiche*. They were about to move on to coffee when Lottie said she'd much rather help clear the kitchen and instructed Philippe to sit down and she and Natalie would quickly do the dishes and then they could all enjoy a coffee together. He was a little taken aback at the direct instruction but Natalie admitted he'd done the lion's share and to sit back and relax with a bit of Martial Solal. They would load the dishwasher, put the coffee on and be back in five minutes. Lottie wasn't too sure who Solal was but soon heard the gentle sound of jazz piano wafting into the kitchen.

The two women set about stacking the dishwasher. Natalie started to prepare the coffee while Lottie carried on with the loading. They worked in an affable harmony for a few minutes until Natalie suddenly announced in English "You know my father really likes you. Thanks for helping him discover his emotions again". Lottie nearly dropped the sticky meat tray in shock which caused Natalie to redden and revert to apologising in French. Lottie reassured her that she had not spoken out of turn and that she was equally fond of her dad who been such a support during the last few weeks.

Natalie carried on in French that she worried her dad would "screw up" as he was not used to being in female company since the divorce and he'd phoned her for advice in the last few weeks. Lottie asked what sort of advice and the young girl declared "oh, the usual stuff like what shirt and jeans to wear". She laughed at the remark and affirmed to Natalie that he always looked lovely and he seemed to have an excellent dress sense unless she was buying all his clothes and she should be praising her instead. Natalie confirmed she was not involved and his artistic traits ensured he always put great colours together. Lottie found herself thinking about the night she'd spent in the safety of Philippe's house. She decided to check whether Natalie had phoned that night. "But of course" she explained. "He had already phoned me to say you were coming over and would his green check shirt work with his navy chinos?" By now, Lottie was trying to put the pieces together when Natalie added "I know you were in the sitting room relaxing and he was in the kitchen when I rang to check how it was going. He can be a total cretin sometimes and I was hoping he had not upset you". She thought about Philippe dropping the mobile like a hot potato and looking flustered when she walked into the kitchen.

She stopped loading the dishwasher, cupped Natalie's face in her hands and planted a kiss on her forehead. Natalie had no idea what this meant. Was it some sort of English custom? She knew there were loads of cultural difference between Britain and France which was why she kept checking whether her father was being careful not to upset this new woman in his life.

The coffee pot declared it had finished as it was one of the Italian stovetop ones that were noisy but produced a wonderful aroma and equally great coffee. They carried the tray back through to the sitting room where Philippe was sprawled on the sofa playing imaginary piano. Whether it was too much red wine or the relief that he was not a conspirator in the books and cocaine she wasn't sure, as she grabbed Philippe's legs and swung them around so they dropped to the floor. He pretended to be surprised as Lottie plonked herself next to him and kissed him on the cheek. Natalie poured the coffee whilst inwardly her heart and scheming brain were doing an imaginary happy dance as they "high fived" her success.

The evening drew to a close and everyone hugged and kissed as farewells were uttered and Natalie suggested they should all get together more often. Philippe accompanied Lottie to her car instructing her to be careful and stay alert for the "*flic*" even though she reckoned she'd seen enough police to last a lifetime. They exchanged kisses again and she dropped the window to wave to them both before setting the car into gear and disappearing down the road. She sang all the way back to the apartment out of relief from such a great evening, realising Philippe knew nothing of the drugs, or maybe just a glass or two too many of the local grape!

She lay in bed replaying the evening and savouring the moment she realised that Natalie had been talking to Philippe when he was preparing their pasta meal that fateful night when she didn't know who she could trust. Her thoughts turned to Bob and whether she was being unfair to even consider a new relationship, then she thought of their children who were all supporting and encouraging her to date again. Not least in the mix came Jill admonishing her for creating barriers to any new emotional contact. Everyone seemed to be signalling a green light and it was only Lottie who seemed to be stuck on red or, at best, amber. She reflected on the evening and the more she considered and contemplated, the more the amber light turned green.

CHAPTER NINE
ART FOR ART'S SAKE, MONEY FOR ....

Back at the station, having been ejected from Brother Vialat's room by the doctor, the two Capitaines and Brigadier-Chef Lepireon dissected the new information gleaned from the injured monk. They reviewed the abbey paperwork noting the orders that were shipped out from their rural retreat. Brief details of the orders had been data entered so they could separate the books from the movement of artefacts which seemed to endorse they went to other abbeys holding exhibitions. The team were looking at invoices noting the regular sale of books to a host of end users, a handful of museums and occasionally to private galleries. They could understand why the *La Galerie d'Art et des Artefacts*" had flagged up as they purchased regularly whereas the other galleries bought books on an infrequent basis.

Brother Vialat had acknowledged the use of the gallery and they wished they had not been removed from pursuing that line of the enquiry by the zealous doctor. The gallery was located further south in Marseille so the Avignon team had agreed to own the search of the premises and Lyon had opted to gain more information from Michel Vialat when interviewing him could recommence. Lepireon had taken a photo of the updated Evidence Board before they had both left the Lyon office to head back to the Vaucluse.

Their priority was now investigating the gallery and the Brigadier-Chef rang ahead to start the paperwork process. Serge Lebrun rang his superior to update him of recent events and request that he stay in Avignon until they had a successful arrest. Given the gallery was in Marseille, where OCRTIS had a division and it was Lebrun's base, he knew it might be a "hard sell". The commandant listened to their update which included the shooting of Brother Vialat and the dissemination of the books to various buyers. He raised a number of his own questions which they both responded to demonstrating they were working as a unified team and meriting the continued expense to keep him at the *Municipale* offices. He told them to get a result within the next few days as he had a number of men out on field duties meaning his budget would soon be going into the red and the Commissaire's office would be crawling all over him.

The two officers hung up and smiled at each other acknowledging they would be still glued together for another week or perhaps less if they could bring the case to a swift conclusion. They met up again the next morning where the judge's letter of authority for the search was already awaiting their arrival on Lepireon's desk. It confirmed the building, the personnel and their vehicles could be searched, and the staff questioned and fingerprinted. They rang the gallery to advise them and confirm the owners would be present being a condition of the search. They asked for their fax number and their email address so that the letter of authority could be transmitted prior to their arrival. It was crucial to the case that everything sat within the laws determined by the State. Although there was an element of bravado in refusing consent, the owners of the gallery knew that they would have to succumb to the inspection.

The gallery owner, Gilles Ducourant, put down the receiver and turned to his wife, Marie-Noelle. He advised that tomorrow morning a team would be searching the gallery, the staff and the company vehicles – perhaps they'd better spend the day ensuring the paperwork was all in order! Whilst they organised the files on the shelves and on their laptops, they had no idea that Lebrun had arranged a round-the-clock watch on the exterior of the premises to ensure nothing untoward left the gallery prior to the search.

Capitaine Lebrun had acquisitioned the plans of the building via the sales act when the Ducourants purchased the gallery. He knew they'd bought it eleven years ago from a Côte d'Azur chain of galleries; the building covered two floors totalling eighty square metres. He felt certain that two Brigadiers from Marseille and the two of them were more than adequate to complete the search. He emailed through the data and arranged an audio-visual connection with the two brigadiers so they could outline the search criteria. Everyone had copies of the floor plans and personal details of the French owners.

Gilles Ducourant was fifty-five and originally from Poitiers in in the region of Nouvelle-Aquitaine. He'd married Marie-Noelle Léa, forty-eight years old and born in Marseille in the Provence-Alpes-Côte d'Azur region. They'd been married thirty years and had one daughter who was twenty-five and severely handicapped. They had acquired the gallery from the renowned chain of *Desmoines et Fils* in 2010 and it was in the sought-after location of the Canebière; a long avenue leading to Marseille's old port. Tax returns showed a healthy growth in the business of 28% since its acquisition. According to tax records, they employed one other member of staff; a woman called Camila Milon Da Silva. They had a home above the beach at Pointe Rouge which current records valued around 1.2 million euros and they had a Galeon Skydeck 510 yacht valued at 900,000 euros. They both ran high-end vehicles and enjoyed a lavish and extravagant lifestyle. Capitaine Lebrun summarised the briefing by noting that basic maths would indicate that money had to be earned by another means unless it had been inherited. There was no evidence of any other business controlled by the Ducourants or any investments in other companies.

The team gathered outside the gallery an hour before the scheduled opening time. They noticed a card advising *"fermeture exceptionnellement aujourd'hui"* which seemed an astute way to deter customers as they couldn't buy anything or while away an hour or two if the gallery was shut. The blinds were drawn across the windows so no part of the interior was visible to inquisitive eyes. Monsieur Ducourant opened the door to the officers and gave them a cursory *"Bonjour Messieurs, dame"* and they reciprocated. Capitaine Lebrun introduced his colleagues and explained how the search would proceed. Gilles Ducourant was expensively attired in a lightweight, handstitched suit and Vuitton buckled velour shoes. He confirmed his wife was upstairs in the office and he introduced them to Madame Milon Da Silva who managed sales and exhibitions. She was sitting at a Louis XVI mahogany writing table which acted as a desk for any sales transactions or enquiries. She proffered a trembling hand to the officers as she inwardly wondered how long she would have to tolerate their presence and was it too soon to pop another valium?

Whilst the Brigadiers searched the ground floor which comprised the gallery, a storeroom, kitchen, and washroom, Lepireon and Lebrun went upstairs to the office which ran the length of the ground floor and was clearly an overflow to the storeroom. Marie-Noelle Ducourant extended her hand in welcome but her smile belied a seething anger which bubbled underneath the surface. She was exquisitely dressed in a simple shift dress with a burst of colour at her neck provided by a Hermès scarf; Lapireon noted a colour co-ordinated Fendi tote bag at her feet which appeared to be this season's collection. Monsieur Ducourant enquired where they would like to start and they confirmed with the files referencing deliveries and sales since the time they had acquired the gallery.

The two senior officers poured over the paperwork looking for anomalies and cross-referencing shipments from the abbey. They requested sales paperwork regarding the tooled leather books and Madame Dourant, who didn't miss a beat given the nature of the request, duly ran a spreadsheet from her laptop listing the reference numbers of the invoices. The two of them worked quietly pouring over the abbey data and checking receipts and sales from the gallery. By late morning they had a significant inconsistency of the quantity of books despatched by the abbey versus the recorded sales. Gilles Ducourant confirmed they had thefts from time to time or perhaps it was an accounting error and the abbey had not sent the correct amount. Lebrun challenged that there would be signs they'd queried the orders and there was nothing in the paperwork from the abbey. What evidence could the owners show them to support they had received insufficient books? They both fell silent and returned to searching for information on their laptops. Capitaine Serge Lebrun challenged why the annual accounts did not show up the anomalies and requested information relating to their accountant. Lepireon also questioned how orders were received and who was responsible for unpacking works or arts and the various artefacts. They confirmed it was a shared responsibility with Madame Milon Da Silva.

The officers descended the stairs to verify the process with her. She quickly became agitated by the questions and threw her hands in the air stating she seldom unpacked goods and she just noted the orders were correct and moved the items to the stockroom. She maintained her involvement in shipments mostly related to exhibitions. She was responsible for ensuring items shipped in perfect condition and validating the returns were complete and undamaged. They acknowledged her explanation and noted her nervous and slightly agitated manner. Lepireon stayed questioning her to build a better profile of her character and role in the gallery.

Towards the end of the day, they moved their search to the vehicles which were in an underground car park. Camila also had a company car although it was a small electric run-around compared to the Ducourants' vehicles. Gilles drove a large 5-door series 6 BMW Gran Tourismo and Marie-Noelle's vehicle of choice was a Mercedes AMG Roadster. There was evidence everywhere pointing to the gallery owners' affluence. They were a well-heeled couple who enjoyed the finer things in life and their sales figures made it difficult to account for the gallery profits supplying these expensive toys and their coastal property.

Pretty much as expected, the cars provided no evidence which lead Capitaine Lebrun to take Lepireon aside and suggest they arrange a search of the home and the yacht the next day. He asked her to contact the Avignon office and arrange the necessary paperwork with the judge indicating that additional searches into the couples' finances were required. They returned to the gallery and advised that the search warrant would be extended to their home and yacht. In the morning, they wanted their accountant to explain how the quantities of orders for tooled leather books did not match the reported sales. They were expecting to see evidence to support the missing books within 24 hours. Lepireon thought Marie-Noelle Ducourant would be washing her hands for days when she saw the volume of ink required for the fingerprints. This action was the first to challenge the cool façade of indifference which she'd managed to maintain all day.

They left the gallery to a civil but rather acerbic "*Au revoir et à demain*" from the Ducourants who did not relish seeing them at their home the next day. The senior officers drove back to Avignon discussing the day's events and dissecting the characters of the three people who had been interviewed. Their years of experience in the police attested that Monsieur and Madame Ducourant were both hiding something but they both felt that their assistant was a nervy but innocent accomplice to their misdoings. They rang Thierry Barreau in Lyon in the hope he had some good news. He certainly did have news as he updated them of a further attempt on Brother Michel Vialat's life.

Brigadier Pillon was on duty outside Vialat's room when a man approached him advising he needed to give a pain killer injection to Brother Vialat. He was dressed as one of the hospital personnel and was clutching a pager which was buzzing in his hand. There was nothing to alert Brigadier Pillon other than he was an unfamiliar face amongst the personnel he now recognised given he'd completed a number of shifts. He allowed the doctor to enter the room but decided to verify what was happening through the glass window. At the same moment, he realised something he'd registered proved this was no medical doctor. Brigadier Pillon rushed into the room where he fought with the intruder and managed to grab the syringe. The pseudo doctor managed to escape the officer even though he gave chase down the hospital's many corridors. A white coat had been found later in a lift on the second floor and they were currently checking the syringe for its contents and any DNA. Evidently what Michel Vialat knew, and who he knew, presented an ongoing risk for the drug runners and the dirty fingernails holding the buzzing pager declared they would go to any length to eradicate him.

Michel Vialat had been moved to another hospital in Lyon and given a false patient identity. For the moment, he was protected and Barreau was going to see him within the hour particularly as Brigadier Pillon was under the impression Vialat knew the bogus doctor. Lebrun reciprocated with his information and explained their search had brought forth a disparity on the number of books received versus the recorded sales and the owners were clearly living above their means. Their one member of staff appeared anxious and highly strung but they both considered these were characteristic traits rather than any degree of culpability. They were moving the search to the Ducourants' house and boat tomorrow to explore their personal finances.

The car swung into the driveway of a grandiose *Maison de Maître* at Point Rouge. It was going to be a stressful day for the team as the Mistral wind was blowing at 110 kilometres per hour and they'd avoided all manner of flying detritus on their route south to Marseille. The manor house's cliff top location only added to the wind's impact and Capitaine Lebrun knew the two brigadiers would get little protection from the harbour when they went to the port to inspect the yacht. The Ducourants were respectful, as they had been yesterday but their smiles didn't match the cold chill in their eyes as they shook hands with the officers. Capitaine Lebrun requested the accountant's feedback on the missing sales but Gilles Ducourant said that he was on holiday in Réunion. He would be in Saint Philippe for another five days and his secretary refused to contact him as he had been unwell for some time and needed a vacation away from the stress and demands of the business. This was disappointing and did not advance the investigation but there was little that Lebrun or Lepireon could do other than reaffirm the information was critical the minute that he returned to the office.

They conducted the search of the building and a small garden guesthouse for friends and family. Lepireon noted that there was no sign of their handicapped daughter living at the house. Madame Ducourant confirmed she was in a residential home as she required around the clock nursing care which she felt unable to provide. Lepireon couldn't put her finger on why this admission unsettled her but she knew she'd recently seen something or read something that challenged this statement. The search moved from material evidence to a fiscal audit so the two Brigadiers were released to go to the port and search the yacht. Serge Lebrun and Aurélie Lepireon requested their personal tax declarations and the "*avis des impositions*" were microscopically examined. Capitaine Lebrun was becoming more and more frustrated by the lack of evidence when every inch of his experience screamed that they were guilty of crimes. Marie-Noelle Ducourant confirmed she was party to a personal inheritance which supplemented their income but Lebrun and Lepireon both found the balance sheet lacking when they delved further into the figures.

They were wrapping up their investigations as Lebrun barked at Gilles Ducourant causing Lepireon to hear the frustration in his voice: *"Écoutez bien, Monsieur et Madame Ducourant, j'ai les co-ordonnées de votre comptable. Son retour est prévu en cinq jours que je peux vérifier avec sa sécretaire. J'insiste qu'il me contacterai au bureau le matin de son retour sinon je prendrai contact avec le Trésor Public. Ce n'est pas fini Monsieur et Madame Ducourant – pas de tout!"* Lepireon took her queue and packed up her briefcase as her colleague momentarily lost his cool and reminded the homeowners that they had just five days before they'd be knocking on the accountant's door or the matter would be passed to France's tax office. Gilles and Marie-Noelle Ducourant concluded they'd suffered enough humiliation during the last forty-eight hours without having France's tax auditors crawl over the paperwork again which would certainly uncover occasional cash payments and, therefore, additional tax charges and fines.

The senior officers drove in silence down the cypress lined entrance and back onto the main road. Before returning to Avignon, Serge Lebrun wanted to get a look at the Skydeck yacht and where exactly it was moored. Port fees alone were an annual eye-watering amount in the Marseille marina. He ran his hand through his hair in frustration at the last two days but his colleague didn't notice. She was lost in her own thoughts trying to recall what it was about the daughter that didn't match to her being in a residential nursing home.

They parked up and walked through the pedestrianised road towards the harbour which was a kaleidoscope of coloured yachts and fishing boats. Some of the quayside restaurants were still serving a few of the tables and Lebrun wondered if they were lingerers from a very late lunch or early clients seeking out an evening meal; either way he was beginning to feel very hungry which didn't enhance his overall mood. One of the brigadiers met them at the *Restaurant des Glycines* and walked them down to the yacht moored on Quay 35. Even though it was dated in comparison to some of the super yachts moored in the port, it was still a striking craft with a decent sized engine. The officers advised they'd spent two hours conducting the search and swabbed most of the areas where fingerprints were visible. They'd lifted prints from the main forward berth and a smaller second berth. They left Lebrun and Lepireon up on deck as they returned to the Ducourants' home with the keys.

The senior officers looked across at the tourists milling into the cafés, restaurants and shops; music carried down the quay as the street musicians serenaded the café goers and the early diners. Lebrun knew Le Vieux Port very well as he lived in a flat just off Avenue de la Corse. Lepireon had been down to the port a few times both on business and socially. The area was, undoubtedly, one of the prettiest ports with an array of tiny fishing boats sharing the crystal blue water with the multi-million-dollar yachts. There were not many sights that summed up the difference between the "haves" and the "have nots" that weren't encapsulated by looking at the variety of marine craft moored off the harbour. She knew that Le Vieux Port had its fair share of evening miscreants who hoped to pick a tourist pocket for a phone, a wallet or even the chance of "lifting" an item of jewellery. She could even see one of her colleagues questioning a gang of teenagers near the cathedral. She looked across at Serge Lebrun and said "home?" and he nodded in agreement realising his apartment was just five minutes' away but the police reserve apartment would have to do.

They walked back to the car mulling over everything that they'd learned today. It was accepted that illegal money was funding the house, yacht and cars. Lepireon explained that something was untoward about the daughter but she couldn't put her finger on what was troubling her. Lebrun queried whether it was something with the paperwork that they'd reviewed over the last two days or something on file at the station? She had no idea but she knew it was significant and pertinent to their investigation.

They drove north in companionable silence and reached the station in a couple of hours due to the heavy evening commuter traffic. They completed the search warrant findings and Lebrun put a call through to the Lyon commissariat. At least they had more positive news as Thierry confirmed the syringe contained a lethal dose of Propranolol which would have stopped Vialat's heart in seconds. They had clear DNA on the white coat and the syringe, and the police database had matched it to a known criminal in the Pas de Calais. He had a couple of prison terms for theft with violence, multiple records of domestic burglary and then all records came to an abrupt halt several years ago.

The weary officers swapped their uniform polo shirts for T-shirts and popped across the road for glass of chilled white wine. They both consumed a dish of large green olives marinated in cumin and harissa spices and Lebrun thought of an evening pizza and Lepireon of a husband who she hoped had prepared their evening meal.

CHAPTER TEN
HOME TRUTHS

Barreau had interviewed Vialat most of the morning requesting details of the sarabaite training which had been conducted at a house in a hamlet thirty minutes from Lyon. Vialat confirmed that they'd been instructed to wear their robes and adopt the mannerisms and characteristics of monks in order they would not draw attention to the building or its purpose. Michel Vialat recognised the man who had come into his hospital room as he'd been one of his fellow trainees. He didn't know his name as they'd been under instruction not to mix with each other and to create aliases should the team ever be investigated at a future date. It was clear to him that this colleague had been ordered to kill him and he would have succeeded if it had not been for the brigadier watching him through the window. Barreau acknowledged his colleague's actions in preventing the man's death confirming Vialat was still not strong enough to overpower the man.

Barreau decided to check in with his Avignon colleagues who were working hard to locate sufficient evidence to bring about an arrest. He could do little more from Lyon other than pursue the sarabaite operation which was now a priority and would hopefully identify a number of criminal monks in monasteries across France. He needed Capitaine Lebrun to agree that his involvement was now reduced to questioning Michel Vialat as and when the need arose. He would be leaving hospital in two days and a safe house had been arranged for a few weeks and then he'd have to cope without police protection. The southern team were driving back up from Marseille and sounded flat and frustrated on the phone call with their colleague. Their forty-eight hours hadn't brought forth the results they wanted other than some accounting issues on receipts versus sales. It was the same old story and Barreau suspected a few back pocket cash sales until he learned of the quantity of anomalies. It would be unusual to lose so many incoming books versus recorded sales. He informed them that he would pursue the larger sarabaite training operation unless they thought there was a conflict or a need for his team. Lebrun accepted that it made sense. The gallery was being fed the books and the drugs but they didn't know their part in the distribution process. It made sense for Barreau to attack the source whilst they continued their investigations in the South.

Lepireon went into the offices the next morning having decided overnight that she would retrace her steps with the files and computer records before they had left the office to conduct the search of Ducourants' gallery. She reviewed the documentation and the interview records and then turned to the computer data. She ploughed on through the criminal records of Jean-Louis Pislait and Michel Vialat. She revisited Madame Pearce's various encounters with the men and then started to look at financial records for the Ducourants. There was a glimmer of hope by the end of the morning when Lebrun announced that Vialat's prints had been found in several areas on the Skydeck yacht. Lebrun phoned this information through to Lyon as Vialat had definitely not mentioned his direct link with the gallery or that he'd visited the boat and stayed in the guest berth. When Thierry Barreau had restarted the interview following the doctor ejecting the team from the room, Vialat had only acknowledged the gallery was a despatch address for the books containing the drugs. Barreau decided to put pressure on him and remove the offer of the safe house and confirm he'd be released out of hospital whereupon he could return to the abbey. He hoped that might refresh his memory and he'd clarify his involvement with the Ducourants.

Lepireon continued her relentless pursuit of the fiscal documents relating to the couple. It was not until she'd been stuck at her computer for over five hours that she suddenly stood up and did a small satisfactory jig of delight combined with a few star-jumps to get her circulation moving again. Lebrun gave her a broad grin looking up optimistically from his terminal as she gave him the excellent news that had been troubling her for twenty-four hours. Six years ago, the Ducourants had purchased a Marseille town house in Rue des Fabres in the name of their daughter, Sophie Ducourant. Why would they do that when she was in a residential home? Had it been a plan to try and renovate the house for their daughter's needs or was it a house that they didn't want to publicise belonged to them? They had made no reference to it during the two days and further records showed that it had not been sold and they were still paying the land tax and occupancy tax on the property. Other than the accounting issue, this building was the best news they'd had in a couple of days. Lebrun congratulated his colleague on her diligence and perseverance as she'd known from the minute Marie-Noelle Ducourant had mentioned the nursing home that something was disturbing about the remark. This time they knew they'd still have to play by the rule book but they would not announce their presence at the address until their arrival in front of the premises. This would not give the Ducourants any opportunity to remove items or refuse access as their gallery was only three parallel streets away from the house; one of them was bound to be nearby. They started the application for a search warrant one more time.

It was a bright sunny day when they drove back down to Marseille where the same Marseillaise brigadiers awaited them given they were now very familiar with the case. Serge Lebrun was in front of the house in Rue des Fabres where the curtains were drawn and there were no obvious signs of activity. He rang Gilles Ducourant's mobile phone and it was picked up within a few rings giving Lebrun the opportunity to ask if he was at the gallery today. He confirmed that he was but there were a handful of clients downstairs so he sincerely hoped the detective was not intending to pay yet another visit. Lebrun broke into a smile and nodded his head at Lepireon in acknowledgement of the response. He asked him to please come to the property in Rue des Fabres whereupon a team of investigators were waiting to conduct a search. There was a painfully long silence and Lebrun interjected "*Monsieur Ducourant?*" Ducourant challenged his authority to notify him so late of the warrant but Lebrun was on safe ground given the potential for illicit drugs on the premises. He said he would have to go to Pointe Rouge first and collect the keys but Lebrun said that a delay was not necessary as they would gain access by breaking the door unless he appeared in ten minutes.

Capitaine Lebrun could only imagine the conversation happening at the gallery offices between the husband-and-wife team. They realised a locked door was no deterrent and Gilles needed to go and give them the key which was sitting on the desk in front of them on his keyring. The couple both knew exactly what they would find and Gilles wondered if he wanted to be physically present at the inspection. Gilles Ducourant drove his car to the property and passed the officers stating he was going to find a place to park. Everyone knew the gallery was within walking distance and it was just a delaying tactic but they had plenty of time. Given the rather derelict façade to the house, Lebrun noted the installation of an alarm box situated near the roof and noted to Lepireon that something was worth protecting in the house. Ducourant returned five minutes later and requested to see the paperwork thereby causing a further delay. The urgent business phone call, which was so important that he insisted he needed to take it, was undoubtedly his wife trying to stall the inevitable. The team took it all in their stride and waited until Ducourant could not think of any further reasons why he should not open the door. They entered the premises together as Gilles disabled the alarm and Lebrun confirmed and registered the code in his notebook. There was an asphyxiating odour of lavender oil causing them to gag slightly and Lepireon to recall her childhood trip to the lavender oil distillery near Apt. In small quantities the perfume from the plant was joyous and had many healing qualities but in larger quantities it could have you choking for breath.

Lebrun asked Gilles Ducourant to accompany him through the house. They had a rough idea of the number of rooms from the plans relating to the purchase of the property but they had no idea if any renovations had been done or exactly what they would find. The ground floor had a large reception room in which there were two temporary wooden trestle tables alongside a handful of boxes. There was a kitchen visible through the doorway and another door led to a cloakroom with a toilet and washbasin. They took the uncarpeted staircase to the first floor where Lebrun's gaze took in the converted bedroom which was now an office with a large wooden bookcase full of files and a portable computer on a desk. They carried on to the upper floor which was clearly abandoned as they could see the trace of their footsteps in the dust that had obviously collected over six years since the purchase of the property. Lepireon took responsibility for the ground floor with the two brigadiers and took the keys from her colleague so she could ensure the front door was locked. Lebrun had responsibility for the office and invited Gilles Ducourant to take a seat. The laptop would be impounded but the files and folders in the bookcase were worth reviewing immediately.

Lebrun took a selection of ring binders from the bookcase and opened them on the desk. The spines of the binders detailed the year and, in just a glance, it was obvious they dated back seven years. The current year showed receipts and invoices for the tooled leather books being copies of what they had seen in the gallery but there were notes alongside most of them and coloured highlighters across descriptions. He took down the previous year and it was the same thing. Some of the lines were highlighted in yellow and others in pink but then he realised the files were full of highlighted lines in a range of colours referencing deliveries in Italy, Sicily and Sardinia. He asked Ducourant what the colour coding meant but he said his wife did the paperwork and he had no idea. Lebrun knew it was a lie but he was optimistic that they were now at the heart of the operation. The documentation held the personal data of a number of contacts and these were dispersed across several European countries. He called the officers to come and collect the files and the laptop causing Ducourant to object until he showed him the warrant again and the paragraph noting the removal of any items deemed of interest.

Lepireon was having an equally productive time investigating the boxes which contained at least forty of the exquisite leather books. There were also some other boxes containing cheap leather replicas that had none of the charm or skilled work of the others. A large bottle of lavender oil and a paintbrush sat next to the boxes which equally reeked of the oil. It was unclear how these items were involved but she certainly recognised the quality books as some that had contained cocaine and the cheaper books as those that were drug free being the type she'd returned to Cédric Mallet. She went up to Lebrun and they conducted a whispered conversation on the staircase as they agreed they had enough to take the Ducourants into custody in Marseille. They decided that there was no evidence to show that Camila Milon Da Silva had any understanding of the activities at Rue des Fabres so they would take the couple to the Commisariat at Marseille. If need be, Lebrun could remain in the city to conduct the interviews, get the cyber team to access the laptop and ascertain any fingerprint evidence on the books.

Lepireon ensured the officers removed all the evidence and then went to the gallery to take Madame Ducourant into custody. She recited the legal reasons for being put under "*garde à vue*" although Madame Ducourant was hitting the phone to talk to her lawyer at the time so the details of Article 3, 2012 were uttered to a woman who obviously wasn't listening to her. Madame Ducourant was busy trying to by-pass a secretary's insistence that Maître Vidal was in a meeting. Back at the house, Lebrun was doing the same with Gilles Ducourant but he seemed reconciled to an imminent personal interrogation whilst his wife was trying her utmost to avoid it. It was a very bad day, very bad indeed.

Back in Lyon, Thierry Barreau was conducting a further interview with the hospital patient. He explained that the safe house was being used and he didn't have another one available, therefore, he'd have to go back to the abbey. As expected, Michel Vialat became anxious, white-faced in fear and declared the senior officer was sending him to his certain death. Barreau advised he had no reason to protect him any more as Vialat was still withholding information. "Quoi?" uttered Vialat providing Barreau the route to question why his fingerprints had been found on the Ducourants' yacht. He slumped back on his pillow and nervously tugged at his eyebrow which Barreau noted he tended to do when faced with a difficult question and he needed to buy some time. He confirmed the evidence spoke for itself with his prints in the guest berth and galley of the boat therefore it was undeniably true that he was familiar with the boat and the Ducourants. He expressed his frustration at Vialat explaining that they could not help him if he continued to hide important information even when his life was being threatened.

Vialat accepted that he no longer wanted to be at risk and he'd already embarked on sharing a lot more information than he had initially wanted to give to the police. Seeing his colleague heading for him with the syringe confirmed that the operation now expected him to confess, or they believed that he would do so in the coming days. He would need the help of the police if he was to survive and create a new future. Michel Vialat looked straight at Barreau and confirmed that he had met the Ducourants several times. He and Jean-Louis usually collected the books and they both split the spines to access the cocaine. Vialat took the bags down to Marseille and frequently met the Ducourants on their boat to handover the cocaine and collect payment which he shared with Jean-Louis. Sometimes, he stayed overnight on the yacht but never with the owners who he knew had a house overlooking the coast. He knew little about them other than they enjoyed a number of holidays and always sailed to their destination of choice, therefore, he assumed these trips were linked to the drugs. Gilles Ducourant was welcoming and hospitable, however, he found Marie-Noelle Ducourant quite the opposite of her husband. She was rude, treated him like a servant and was usually critical of him staying overnight on the boat. Barreau listened intently as he quickly wrote down Vialat's relationship with the Ducourants. He asked about finding the drugs in the mausoleum on the abbey grounds and Vialat explained that he'd panicked. As sacrist, and a person of trust, the abbot had alerted him to the search of the premises. He'd previously stored the bags of cocaine in his private quarters but he'd realised that it was imperative to find a new location and to find it fast. The mausoleum seemed a logical choice as nobody would lift the stone lid of the founder abbot. They exchanged looks that confirmed life didn't always go to plan!

Barreau preferred not to divulge to Vialat that an eight-man team and dog handler were scheduled for a raid on the training centre in the morning. He was a wily character who only fed information once he was cornered with evidence and he didn't trust him not to contact the education centre. Instead, Thierry rang through the latest update to Serge Lebrun who duly noted the new information and they found themselves wondering where the money was stored. He and Barreau agreed that there must be money from the drug dealing lying in a strongbox or vault – but where? It must be many thousands as they had to pay Vialat and Jean-Louis at regular intervals and they had their lifestyle to maintain. Had they missed something at the gallery, the houses or the yacht? Lebrun knew they'd crawled all over the house at Pointe Rouge and the two officers had been extremely diligent searching the yacht. Maybe the success of finding the files and books at the house had detracted him from searching for money? He hoped the test results on the books would be back shortly but, in the meantime, he was still within the search warrant's authorised hours so he gathered up Ducourant's keyring and headed back to the house in Rue des Fabres with Lepireon.

The structure of the house had not been altered since the day of purchase and it was devoid of furnishings and knick-knacks as it had been acquired for just one reason and that was not for their daughter. They were looking for all the usual places where a person would store cash. The only room that was carpeted was the sitting room which had a threadbare and stained wall-to-wall covering undoubtedly left by the previous owners. They effortlessly pulled it up exposing a concrete floor so continued in silence exploring the rest of the room. They moved into the kitchen and thoroughly searched it again short of prising the kitchen units from the walls. They both felt that any cash would be readily accessible and there would have been signs of damage if fixtures had to be broken at regular intervals. The two of them checked out the small cloakroom housing a washbasin and toilet but, short of finding cash in the cistern, they accepted it was not looking hopeful so far. Both of them looked upwards at the greying, polystyrene tiled ceiling which was pretty flimsy and had stains and grime across the previously white tiles. In the absence of a stepladder, Lebrun suggested Lepireon climb onto his shoulders causing her to regard him warily and mutter under her breath. He crouched down and she clambered onto his body steadying herself by grabbing his hair. He yelled at her telling her to take it easy as alopecia ran in his family. She started giggling and it took a few minutes wobbling on his shoulders for her to gather herself and reach up to remove one of the polystyrene tiles. She ended up removing all of them so they were both covered in the dirt and crud that dropped down from the opening. They were looking up at a cement screed of the upper floor so the acrobatics had been in vain.

They both ended up in the office stamping a staccato danse on the wooden floorboards in the hope there might be some that were loose or had been removed. There was little else in the room other than the pine bookcase, the desk which had held the laptop computer and the faded blue curtains. Serge Lebrun looked at the empty bookcase that had previously been full of folders and asked Lepireon to give him a hand as he started to pull it away from the wall. They realised it was on felt feet as it slid effortlessly and quietly across the floor clearly exposing a *Fichet* wall safe and they looked at each other with congratulatory, smug faces. Fortunately, it was not a digital safe that required a code and they checked the keys on Gilles Ducourant's keyring until they got lucky with the penultimate one. They opened the safe which contained a stash of envelopes bursting with euro notes of mixed denominations together with two cheap mobile phones. Lepireon removed her gloves and took a fresh pair from her bag. She lifted out the envelopes and the phones and placed them in an evidence bag. At a rough guess there was probably just over a million euros that had been sitting behind the files and the Ducourants would be pretty upset to know that the safe and its contents had just been discovered.

They returned to the station where Capitaine Lebrun received notification that the tooled books contained cocaine; the replica leather books were narcotic free. He was informed that one of the computer brains had gained access into the laptop and was currently trying to break into Gilles Ducourant's email traffic. Lebrun and Lepireon acknowledged the information and Serge requested a discrete surveillance be placed on Rue des Fabres in case anyone else was involved in the trafficking and using the premises. He also invited one of his colleagues to join him in an interview room where the three of them counted the envelopes of cash and discovered there was 1.4 million euros. It was taken to the Security Department, where the receiving officer verified the amount, and the paperwork was completed to transfer it to the judicial system who would hold the funds until a court hearing. They returned to interview room SE1 where he swiftly outlined the case and the players and requested the detective's assistance in the interview of Gilles Ducourant. Brigadier-Chef Lepireon was heading to a cell where Marie-Noelle Ducourant was sitting on the horsehair mattress clutching her handbag to her chest and sporting the frosty expression that she'd not dropped from the minute Lepireon arrested her.

The notaire, Maître Vidal, arrived within a half hour of her phone call and was asking to see either of his clients. The Ducourants had always been most generous to him and it seemed they both needed his assistance at the moment as they were under arrest which beggared belief. He needed to understand the charges and demanded to speak to the arresting officer resulting in Lebrun coming to the reception area to update him on the case. He was totally stunned by the news; the Ducourants and drugs how could this be possible? Vidal suggested he should contact the office if Capitaine Lebrun wanted to interview the Ducourants at the same time as he would need one of his colleagues to attend. Lebrun advised it would not be necessary as Madame Ducourant was currently in a cell and they would commence with Monsieur Ducourant. He kept muttering under his breath *"ce n'est pas possible"* as Lebrun escorted him to the interview room to await his client.

Serge Lebrun opened the interview with Gilles Ducourant stressing he was under caution and explaining the consequences of trafficking cocaine and the many years of imprisonment that would certainly follow. He stressed the Ducourants' lives would be over by the time they came out of prison and their daughter effectively "orphaned" during their confinement. There was nothing that could alter the outcome, however, the number of years could be affected by his ability to help them and his cooperation during the interview. Firstly, his willingness in explaining the drug trafficking operation and, secondly, his help in bringing the sarabaite activity to justice. Gilles Ducourant challenged the second point as he has no idea what the detective was talking about and he muttered a few words into the ear of Maître Vidal.

Lebrun dismissed the protestations and proceeded to the death of Jean-Louis Pislait. Gilles Ducourant's phone records proved he had been talking to Michel Vialat in Rue de la Republique in Avignon just seconds before his death. Michel Vialat had confirmed that he was receiving instructions to end Pislait's life and had the choice of either doing as instructed or he'd be murdered himself. Lebrun confirmed that Gilles Ducourant was the person giving these instructions to murder the man. He shot out of his chair uttering *"ce n'est pas vrai, l'idée est ridicule Monsieur"* only causing Lebrun to bellow *"Asseyez-vous Monsieur Ducourant"* as the man shook his head violently declaring he and Vialat had been friends for years and it wasn't possible that he'd do such a wicked thing and he had not instructed him to take any action against Pislait. This caused the detective to produce the CCTV image of Vialat pushing his friend under the truck and some gruesome photos of Pislait under the truck which the solicitor regarded in horror. Both men shuddered in disbelief and averted their eyes from the images. The detective alongside Lebrun instructed Ducourant to look at the photos reminding him that this was his friend who was murdering a man on his instruction. Gilles looked at them both in amazement and disbelief and refuted the accusation turning to his solicitor and declaring that it simply was not true.

Lebrun addressed the solicitor advising that phone records, together with a signal from a nearby phone tower, proved that his client and Michel Vialat were in dialogue at the time of Jean-Louis Pislait's death. The images of the dead man were once more pushed across the desk and, once more, they both recoiled at the sight of the crushed body. Vidal argued that many people were probably on mobile phones in that very street in Avignon at the time and the phone records proved nothing. Gilles Ducourant nodded his head vehemently in agreement with the statement. Lebrun acknowledged the possibility however, unfortunately, Vialat had left a message on Ducourant's phone following the incident to confirm the instructions had been "carried out". Regrettably, Monsieur Ducourant was now having a problem recalling the instructions that his colleague, Monsieur Vialat, was referencing and what exactly had been "carried out". Given that Monsieur Ducourant acknowledged knowing Vialat, who had visited his yacht on several occasions, the temporary loss of memory was a cause for concern.

A silence fell across the room as the questioning turned to the books and the movement of the drugs. Gilles denied all knowledge of any involvement and began a convoluted story of how the property was being rented to someone else. He had no idea what the tenant did with the house as they were trusting owners who preferred not to interfere with the day-to-day activity of their renters. Lebrun asked the name of the person renting Rue des Fabres causing Ducourant to try and invent a name. The only people who sprang to mind were friends he already knew; the last thing he needed to do was incriminate them. He stalled saying it was a student type he'd met in a bar near the gallery so the kid's name would be on rental paperwork back at the office. The futility of this idea caused his voice to trail off in despair as he eyed Lebrun in the hope that he might accept such an implausible idea. The detective pointed out that no paperwork had been forthcoming in their search and it was a pile of lies given he'd not mentioned it at the gallery or during the search of their home. He'd also made no reference to the student during the search at the house earlier that morning which would have been an excellent time to declare a tenant. Gilles fell silent and realised that he couldn't extricate himself from the discovery of the drugs at the house. He needed to ensure he was not found guilty of the murder of Pislait which was certainly not his fault and tried to steer Lebrun back to Vialat.

The second detective announced that two attempts had been made on Brother Vialat's life owing to him cooperating with their enquiries and that he was now seeking personal protection. Gilles Ducourant appeared genuinely surprised by this news and asked when and how the attempts had been made. Lebrun said he'd been shot and hospitalised and there had been a subsequent attack whilst he was in the hospital. Lebrun studied Ducourant's face and something about his demeanour conveyed that he was possibly not party to this information. It was true that Vialat has recognised his assassin as a trainee sarabaite monk so was it possible that there was no link other than Pislait and Vialat between the two operations?

Gilles was rapidly trying to assess how much evidence they had of the cocaine and his degree of involvement. He decided that it would be impossible to deny his role in the drugs and maybe there was some mileage in cooperating. He needed to get their confirmation of a reduced sentence and challenged them to put on record that he would cooperate if he received a reduction in punishment. Vidal cut across him as he whispered in his ear that he was unclear of the findings at the house so should they request some private time together? Lebrun advised any reduction would be subject to his disclosures relating to Pislait's death and the drug operation, however, it was ultimately a court's decision. Any assistance he offered during the interview might well be viewed in a positive light. Gilles accepted the information as he leant back in the rock-hard plastic chair in defeat. Running his fingers through his raven, dyed hair, he confirmed that Vialat usually brought the drugs to Marseille. He usually met him at the yacht as he preferred meeting him off site from the gallery or his home as Marie-Noelle didn't like him. Lebrun noted that this confirmed what Barreau had also learned from Vialat so there was a chance of some reliable information in amongst the lies. Vidal was doing his best to stop his client from digging an even bigger hole for himself and was constantly cutting across the interview to consult with Gilles in a hushed exchange but it was clear his client appeared defeated.

Lebrun was framing the next question when the door opened and he was passed a note by a colleague. He switched off the recorder, having accepted a pause in the questioning, as both men stood up making their excuses and exiting the room; a brigadier stepped in to assume responsibility of the room's occupant. Camila Milon da Silva was on the phone insisting she be updated on the release of the Ducourants and demanding to know what was happening to her employers. Normally Gilles Ducourant visited his daughter in the nursing home every week and he'd not turned up today. His daughter, Sophie, had been extremely distressed by his absence and had started harming herself. The home had given her a very mild sedative but they were enquiring as to her father's movements. She was notified that the gallery owners would both be held in custody until a court hearing so she would need to advise the home. She naturally jumped on this news asking what was to become of her or the gallery. Lebrun could not answer and only reiterated that they were being held on a very serious crime. She insisted on speaking to them but her request was bluntly denied by Lebrun who advised it was unlikely they would return to the gallery in the immediate future. Camila hung up in a daze. Jesus, what did the detective mean when he said they'd not be back for a while? What crime could they have committed? The morning of the gallery search, she'd overheard a problem about missing shipments but Gilles and Marie-Noelle had said it was nothing important and their accountant would sort it out. Their response to the house search confirmed that it was just another annoyance which they had needed to tolerate.

She knew something had happened this morning as Gilles had rushed out of the gallery saying he was going to the port and he'd looked furious but also like he might throw up at any minute. She'd tried to speak to Marie-Noelle about an upcoming exhibition but she'd bitten her head off screaming at her to leave her alone. She sat back and thought about what she could say to the nursing home regarding Gilles' absence. She'd never been very creative which would have been a useful trait in the current dilemma as she anguished about the daughter. She didn't know Sophie Ducourant but the thought that she was missing her father so much that she was hurting herself struck a chord. Camila had self-harmed for years following her parents' divorce. She knew little about the daughter other than Gilles diligently visited her every week. Marie-Noelle had never visited her since placing her in the home some months ago.

Lebrun went back to the interview room. He realised he now had a possible "way in" to break down Gilles Ducourant who was starting to recognise he was a beaten man. The two officers returned to the room, reconnected the tape and informed Vidal and Ducourant that Camila had been on the phone advising the nursing home had been forced to sedate his daughter. He had been due at the home this morning on his weekly visit and his daughter had not understood why her father had not turned up. She was harming herself so much that the home had taken evasive action and sedated her. Gilles Ducourant leapt out of his chair and insisted he be taken to the nursing home immediately. *"Asseyez-vous!"* barked Lebrun for the second time as Gilles sat back down in shock as his eyes pleaded with Maître Vidal to intervene and he started wringing his hands and muttering under his breath. Just in case there was any misunderstanding by his detainee, Lebrun confirmed that their bank accounts were now frozen and all transactions were halted. He explained it would not take long before the nursing home would realise their bills were not being paid and they would clearly not support looking after Sophie Ducourant without payment. Had her father not considered that his daughter would soon be transferred to a state-run nursing home with none of the comforts that their daughter clearly enjoyed at the current facility? Lebrun pressed on advising their house search had uncovered invoices highlighting the exemplary level of care she was being offered. In that care, they provided several additional activities such as physio, horse-riding, music therapy, painting and these were all noted as supplementary charges. These benefits might be lost as she would not receive the same degree of mental and physical stimulation at a state institution.

Gilles Ducourant couldn't tolerate hearing any more about a reduction of his daughter's living conditions and medical care. He looked submissively at Lebrun and his colleague and uttered *"Que voulez-vous savoir?"* Vidal quickly cut across his client's offer of assistance suggesting instead that they discuss the matter of his daughter's future care. Gilles slumped down in the chair once more clearly heartbroken and crushed. He refused Vidal's offer and turned to the two officers. He needed to avoid any murder charge but the drugs trafficking was far too complicated to avoid given the existing evidence at Rue des Fabres. He needed to get the financial constraints lifted to pay Sophie's bills which was his top priority even if he and Marie-Noelle were in prison.

He knew his wife would have a completely different point of view as her "imperfect child" was just an embarrassment and they'd never agreed on anything regarding their daughter. The endless rows every day had only stopped when he'd moved her to the home although she then complained about the cost to them both in supporting Sophie's monthly bills. The rows had previously been about managing her day-to-day care so it struck Gilles that she would always complain about their challenging daughter as she had done since her birth all those years ago; there was not an ounce of maternal compassion. He didn't doubt that his wife was being totally uncooperative if someone was interviewing her right now, however, she'd be dismayed and possibly kill him if she realised he was about to explain the events of the last seven years.

He dismissed Vidal who realised he would be unable to help Gilles Ducourant any further if he was intent on confessing all. He was fully prepared to "fall on his sword" for his daughter and he thought of his own family and knew he would do exactly the same. He would be wrong to challenge his decision or the need to put his daughter's care as his top priority. Unfortunately, Marie-Noelle Ducourant would not share her husband's caring and thoughtful actions regarding their daughter nor would she have the same degree of emotional worry for her future. He already knew from Gilles that she had blocked the costly renovations at Rue des Fabres which he'd hoped would give Sophie some independence. She was far more calculating in her decisions and he could find little sympathy for her. Even so, he returned to his duty of care to his client and asked to be allowed to speak to Madame Ducourant who was stewing in her cell.

Once Lepireon heard that Vidal was free to support Madame Ducourant, she asked for her to be brought up to the interview room where she was joined by a fellow detective. She was taken to SE2 where she was completely ignorant of the fact her husband had rejected any form of legal assistance. The officers were not prepared to leave the room so Vidal was forced to whisper an update that her husband had received distressing news about their daughter and had selected to cooperate fully with police enquiries. He had refused his legal counsel and the police had acknowledged their questioning would continue without legal assistance which had received his consent.

She didn't take the news well. She started shouting to see her husband immediately and that they had no right to hold them separately. It was all nonsense but they let her rant and scream until she exhausted herself. Vidal did his best to calm her during the outburst which brought no reaction from her interviewers as they'd seen it all before. She turned to him whispering details of the search of the premises in Rue des Fabres that morning, an address he recalled from the purchase of the property some years ago. She advised that incriminating evidence might have been found at the property and she was happy to refuse to answer any questions but was extremely worried that her husband would be tempted to disclose the unfortunate illicit operation which they controlled from the premises. The rotund Monsieur Vidal tugged on his black moustache as he considered this news. It was true that Madame Ducourant had a cold, business-like manner whereas Monsieur Ducourant was always the one who appeared to be the more reasonable and understanding of the pair. What exactly had been found at the property and how was he able to help one half of a partnership when he sensed Gilles Ducourant was already confessing all in a room down the corridor?

The detective accompanying Lepireon began the interview in the same manner as her counterpart in SE1 by highlighting the interview was being conducted under caution and advising of the benefits of cooperation and the possibility of gaining a reduction in sentence. It cut no ice with the woman in front of her whose main concern was for her idiot husband and precisely what he might be disclosing at this time. She hadn't trusted him to hold his tongue particularly if he'd been fed some line about the mutual benefit of helping them with the case and their solicitor had now confirmed he was happily coughing up all he knew. Could it get any worse? They'd spent years building up the cocaine business and she knew they would have found evidence at the house, however, a good lawyer would hopefully help her out of this mess and she pondered whether Maître Vidal was legally astute enough to get her off the charges. She wished she'd had a chance to talk to Gilles before they'd been arrested. He'd been in such a rush to get to Rue des Fabres that she kicked herself for not telling him what to say and what to do. He always thought he knew best but he would never have had the acumen to arrange the narcotics connections let alone turn it into a successful business that they'd both enjoyed for several years. She had provided a life of luxury for them both and it was her links with the sarabaites who had created and developed this business. At least Gilles had no idea that her brother successfully controlled the sarabaite operation as her fool of a husband had the ability to bring them both down together with the bigger prize. During the time sitting in the cell, she had considered different role plays of the interview and settled on a response that she thought might work.

Having confirmed the impact of assisting the police, Lepireon and her colleague began the interview with Madame Ducourant. Neither of the officers were surprised that she maintained her silence and refused to answer their questions with anything other than the French equivalent of "no comment". They introduced aspects of her husband's earlier admissions but she remained resolute and the minutes added up with little advancement until they both decided hearing "*je n'ai rien à dire*" was pointless. She was returned to the cells where she was stripped of her handbag and personal effects. Lepireon suggested she used the waiting time to good effect and reflect on reducing her years in prison as this was certainly going to be her next destination. Marie-Noelle just glared at her and uttered the French equivalent of "piss off, bitch". The metal door slammed shut and Marie-Noelle Ducourant lay on the uncomfortable mattress once more and considered Pislait's stupidity at not collecting the books which would now be party to her downfall. She smiled in delight that at least he was dead thanks to her removing her vacillating husband out of the equation.

In SE1, Gilles Ducourant was considering how best to explain their seven years of extravagance and wondering how he had got caught up in his wife's lies which would end in his prison sentence. In the same moment, in a secure cell, Marie-Noelle Ducourant was working out how to lay all the blame on her birdbrained husband.

CHAPTER ELEVEN
THE ROOT OF THE CASE

Back in Lyon, Thierry Barreau held one last briefing before his team set off for the sarabaite's training centre. They had little information other than the building's structure so there was more than an element of the unknown as they headed to the location. How many trainees would be there, who made up the management team and how many would be present, would they be met with aggression? Thierry didn't have any answers to the questions rattling around in his head and realised that he would just have to follow police procedures in the hope that all the questions were answered before the end of the raid. Brother Vialat was correct in his description as the centre was in a tiny hamlet stuck out in the wilderness which meant they arrived to distant church bells chiming nine o'clock by the time they cleared the heavy Lyon traffic. The building was housed behind a stone wall densely shrouded with dark green laurel bushes. A stone path was visible through the rails of the gate which was padlocked and a shiny chrome interphone on the right of the gate looked out of place in this tiny hamlet that had just a handful of houses surrounded by vines. Barreau pressed the button and announced their arrival and the team, still in their vans, waited until he acknowledged they could descend.

A monk shuffled down the path clutching a selection of keys and looked at the man in front of him at the gate. They deterred visitors and never answered the intercom to couriers and temporary post office personnel looking for a certain address. The declaration of the presence of Capitaine Thierry Barreau, of the Police Nationale, was sufficiently alarming to create a chaotic scene in the boss's office as he scurried around in panic trying to hide files and scattered paperwork. The monk talked to Barreau through the unlocked gate resulting in the officer passing the search documents through the gate for his perusal. It was clear that the brother was considering how best to defer the search and allow his colleagues to tidy or dispose of any incriminating documentation as he painstakingly read each word of the warrant. The monk's procrastination caused Barreau to cut across his examination and request he open the gate immediately or there would be consequences for him and anyone at the property. He reluctantly stuck the key in the padlock and opened the gate giving Barreau the opportunity to click his fingers in instruction for his team to descend their vehicles and the dog handler to release his charge from the rear of the van. They gathered behind Barreau as he followed the monk up the path to the property.

Barreau was fascinated at the monk's character change as he aggressively barked "*attendez*" at them as he scurried off down a corridor. The instruction fell on deaf ears as they followed the rapidly disappearing monk as one large dart intent on hitting its target. As a door flew open, the monk was excitedly declaring to a senior that there were police "all over the building" and they had a search warrant. Their gaze fell upon a plaster, hand-painted mannequin dressed in a monk's cuculla before they spotted a man, dressed in a polo shirt and trousers surveying the gathering of police officers at his office door. He invited them into the room with a warm, calculating smile which remain fixed as

178

Barreau instructed him to read the documentation held by his colleague confirming the property and outbuildings would undergo a search based on information supporting narcotics distribution. Given the reference to narcotics, he may or may not be aware that no warning was necessary of their visit. Barreau waited for the laughter to subside and then requested the name of the man in front of him and his role at the property.

He confirmed he was Georges Léa and he was the Managing Director of the training company. Thierry explained that he had found no company registered at the property so could he explain how he could be the director of a business that appeared to be unregistered and had not submitted any tax declarations. Georges Léa didn't miss a beat as he explained it was a new operation and they were approved to trade temporarily until they received the formal registration paperwork. Barreau requested to know how many people were at the property and recorded fifteen in his notebook. He then asked what they did and waited as Georges Léa confirmed it was an introductory centre to the brotherhood and that anyone interested in becoming a monk or joining the priesthood could explore their vocation through their various classes they offered. Many of their attendees found the training highlighted how isolating and restrictive a life in the brotherhood could be and subsequently opted to pursue other avenues. Léa ended his citation with a simpering smile inwardly congratulating himself on his textbook reply.

Barreau requested that all persons at the property gather in one room within the next five minutes and be available for interview. Léa instructed the monk to call all members into the Dining Room which he duly acknowledged and sped off in the company of two brigadiers requesting to know where to find the temporary interview base. The detective and the rest of his men would conduct a search of the property and he and one of the brigadiers would conduct the interviews. In the meantime, Barreau would start the search himself and it would begin in this office.

Georges Léa confirmed he understood as Barreau reaffirmed the search instructions to his team that had been outlined that morning and they disbanded to head off to the various rooms and levels in the house. What Léa didn't know was the image of Avignon's Evidence Board that was ringing loud bells in Thierry's head as he recalled his southern friends were interviewing and searching the properties of Gilles Ducourant and his wife, born Marie-Noelle Léa. Was there a connection with this man, Georges? He left the office briefly so he could ring the security department and asked them to verify with Vialat at the safe house. In the meantime, maybe he would find documentation to show a relationship with the Ducourants.

The search of the office raised questions about the company as it was unclear how and where the business advertised their services. There appeared to be no invoicing other than to trainers and they could find no evidence of payments from trainees. The business appeared to be operating as a charity with no obvious funding and yet there were fifteen people currently either delivering training or being trained. Capitaine Barreau asked Georges Léa to explain the anomaly and he dismissed the question confirming they had only recently started the business. Barreau asked to see the engagement contracts arranged with the trainers who must be receiving a salary and Léa produced them from a folder noting "Trainers" but the signed contracts were dated with the dates running from the last month up to two years ago.

It was no surprise that the old contracts would raise the question of proof of salary. Léa confirmed they were paid cash whilst they were in the start-up phase and the dates were clearly an error by the individual trainers. It was like a game of tennis with Barreau hitting the serve and Léa smashing a high lob over the net causing Barreau to scrabble to keep the game in play. He had no idea that the suave man in front of him had re-run an unexpected visit by the police in his head and had been practising for this moment for several years. His suspect was perfectly scripted and ready for any searching questions. The trainers knew to acknowledge incorrect dates on their contracts and were only too happy to pocket the cash every month and not have to declare anything to the tax office.

Thierry Barreau could see that Léa's responses would revolve around a new business so he decided to change tack and requested proof of the company's documentation with the Chamber of Commerce for the formation of a training business. A further folder was produced and this contained evidence of a meeting held in the previous month and a business plan. Barreau noted the details and requested to use the phone. Georges Léa became momentarily agitated but pushed his phone across to the detective who punched in the phone number and waited.

Eventually, the detective reached the correct department and requested confirmation of the meeting held with Georges Léa the previous month. Unsurprisingly, they couldn't find any record of the meeting and then checked their archive records which identified the meeting had been held four years ago. Barreau asked them to reaffirm the date which was further confirmed as four years and three months from today's date. The office had recorded the meeting had taken place as an exploratory start-up of a new business and a Monsieur Georges Léa had requested the appointment to verify the process and procedures in creating a company. He hung up and faced Léa who had heard most of the conversation and was rapidly thinking of his next move as he'd not anticipated anyone bothering to check with the CCI. Capitaine Barreau threw the folder onto the desk and asked why he had forged the dates on the documentation causing Georges to bemoan the complexities and hassle of creating a company in France and they'd not got around to putting the business on a formal footing. As much as Barreau recognised the hurdles for entrepreneurs, it was no excuse for totally disregarding the system and trying to operate under the radar of the *Trésor*.

With the cover story blown, the detective challenged how the business could operate and how the trainers were paid for their services? He was genuinely alarmed to hear that the trainers were paid by the trainees which was a bizarre infraction of trading rules and he suspected this had been happening for years given Vialat's description of engaging Jean-Louis Pislait which had been several years ago. This unorthodox business and the Managing Director were clearly marching to the beat of a different drummer and the evidence was building nicely without even conducting the interviews.

Léa watched as the detective made copious notes in his small book whilst one of his colleagues was searching through the drawers and cupboards. There were two laptops in the office and Barreau seized and bagged both of them advising the computers would be held as part of the investigation. He knew he'd be unlikely to find records of the names of monks and the abbeys they had infiltrated for their illegal activities on the laptops unless they were very lucky or Georges Léa was very stupid. Nothing about the character in front of him conveyed a lack of intelligence, quite the opposite. It was far more feasible the information would be on a separate hard drive or even a USB key. There must be reason to review the information from time to time, therefore, a device would be somewhere in the building … but where?

Barreau assisted his colleague as they inspected, probed and prodded in an orderly fashion whilst leaving no evidence of their rummaging so that the office remained in its original condition. Other than the laptops and the unorthodox trading style of the company, they were finding nothing of interest. They both turned their attention to the "silent" occupant in the room, the mannequin. It seemed out of place in the office environment but Georges Léa informed them that all members wore the cuculla on entering training as it would remain their uniform in life and he had the mannequin as part of the interview process and to gauge the correct size of habit for each recruit. He had an answer for everything and it did not go unnoticed by the detective who was beginning to sense the scenario had been rehearsed many times. The mannequin was so old fashioned as to be one of the old plaster built articulated versions where hands and feet were all separate parts in addition to the arms and legs. It was a relic of history and could easily have been a collector's item amongst its fibreglass and plastic counterparts. They undressed the body and removed all the detachable parts. Léa feigned some pressing business matter as he picked up a file and started dictating a letter into a personal recorder whilst all the time eyeing their progress in disdain. The detective noted the distraction of Léa creating a change in the room which he remembered as a key lesson from his training years ago. Their interaction with the mannequin was creating discomfort in Léa and he started to shake every body part with renewed vigour.

It was his fellow brigadier who was forcibly shaking the left hand when they eventually heard the plop of something fall onto the tiled floor causing the voice dictating the letter to stop mid-sentence and turn to face them. Barreau bent to pick up the silver device and instinctively knew to pull it apart. It was a USB key and he removed one of the laptops from the bag and instructed the uncomfortable Managing Director to boot it up whilst he verbally checked and recorded the password in his notebook. The key held an assortment of spreadsheets and letters and Thierry opted to click on a folder marked "Members" and "Current". Bingo! Here he had a list of names and personal data together with the name of the abbey where they were located. It was clear there were also archive records but the urgency was to know who was operating in the religious institutions right now and bring their criminal activities to a swift conclusion.

Thierry Barreau stared at the laptop and then at Georges Léa uttering just one word "*expliquez?*" For the first time since they had arrived, the affable façade disappeared and the detective heard his first "*je n'ai rien à dire*". Fortunately, there was enough evidence to take everyone at the centre into custody to avoid any further opportunity of people ringing or texting through warnings of the raid. It was inevitable the alarm would have already been triggered, therefore, it was imperative to contain any communication to a minimum. Thierry left the office and went down to the corridor to a room where he could hear activity. He found a gathering of robed men amongst his officers and updated one of his colleagues that he would arrange transport for everyone to be taken to the station given the findings so far. It would be easier to manage the interviews whilst they were all under arrest rather than conduct them at the house. The senior brigadier confirmed the change in procedure and passed a box of mobile phones to his boss that had been seized from the gathered brotherhood.

The detective went down various corridors until he found a staircase leading to the upper floors of the house where he found the brigadiers and requested an update on their progress. In some of the dormitories on the first floor, the dog had located cannabis and one of the beds contained heroin in the mattress. The officers had seized two knives and one pistol with ammunition. They had one floor left to search and Barreau updated them on the change of plan to remove the monks to the station for questioning and was exiting the room when his phone rang. He received confirmation that the transport had been despatched and would be with them in a half hour and the Communications Desk advised that the relationship between Marie-Noelle Léa and Georges Léa was sister/brother. The detective acknowledged the link and asked for Capitaine Lebrun in the Marseille office to be made aware of this link with the Ducourants. He returned to the office on the ground floor and updated Georges Léa that he, together with all personnel, would be taken to the station for questioning causing the Managing Director to challenge the grounds for his clients and staff to be removed from their place of work. Knowing there would be plenty of other reasons which would unfold, the detective advised they would begin with "business malpractice" causing the arrested man to physically deflate in front of him and the earlier bravado and arrogance dissipate like a popped balloon.

The detective gathered up the laptops and USB stick and confirmed he would be heading to the station. Brigadier Dufoy would be the senior in charge until the search had been completed and the transport had arrived to remove the personnel to the station. He thanked the team in the Dining Room for their support and professionalism and headed out to his car having already started to punch in the phone number of Serge Lebrun on his phone.

CHAPTER TWELVE
BUSINESS OR PLEASURE?

Lebrun and his colleague were pursuing further details with Gilles when they heard a colleague's knock on the door. Apparently, Maître Vidal needed a few minutes' dialogue with his client. It took only a few seconds for Vidal to realise that Madame Ducourant's assessment was correct as Gilles had already acknowledged his participation in the drugs located at the house and the role of the two monks. He was refuting the murder charge causing Vidal to acknowledge there was already some extremely incriminating evidence and he couldn't turn back the clock on what had already been admitted on tape in front of the two officers. He now needed to help his client on the murder charge otherwise another twenty-five to thirty years were going to be added to his sentence. He invited the officers to continue but could they please specifically address the matter of the murder of Jean-Louis Pislait as his client was innocent of any involvement. By now Maître Vidal was beginning to question whether the man alongside him could be guilty of manslaughter even if dealings to date with Monsieur Ducourant appeared to demonstrate that he was of good character.

Brigadier-Chef Lepireon knocked on the door of interview room SE1. Lebrun's fellow detective couldn't mask the frustration of the interruptions as he greeted Brigadier-Chef Lepireon. She whispered to Serge Lebrun that Marie-

Noelle was continuing to stonewall them and maybe her time was best served helping him as she was now back in a cell. He agreed and she pulled up a chair.

Capitaine Lebrun appraised Gilles Ducourant of the information they had gleaned from Michel Vialat and the team recorded his confirmation that the drugs arrived via the tooled leather books which were collected by the monks and the drugs were extricated from the spines for validation by him and his wife. There were many unscrupulous dealers out there who sent poor quality product so they found they always had to ascertain the quality of the cocaine. They retained the books and did makeshift repairs on them as they were still needed for the distribution process. Lebrun continued detailing Vialat's confession that he brought the drugs to the port of Marseille at regular intervals, however, Capitaine Lebrun was interested to know why the number of deliveries to Monsieur Mallet had recently increased and could he explain this change in frequency? *"Normalement, les livraisons étaient chaque mois et de temps en temps il y avait des livraisons "blancs"* he advised confirming that the deliveries were monthly with an occasional clean shipment of just books. The schedule had been increased once the books had been taken by the British woman as he and his wife had been worried the arrangement was now at risk. He confirmed the "missing sales evidence" which had been highlighted at the gallery search were the books containing the drugs which they'd located at Rue des Fabres. It was a shame they hadn't thought to have the books copied so they could be resold. The two detectives recorded their agreement on tape indicating the anomaly had put the missing books under a spotlight.

The solicitor sat quietly awaiting an opportunity to denounce his client's involvement in the murder of Jean-Louis Pislait. He had already authorised the ongoing interview without his presence so he had no grounds to cut across the unravelling confession.

Lepireon challenged how a relationship had started with the two monks. Gilles Ducourant did not know as it seemed that they'd always been part of the system of receiving the packages and bringing them to Marseille. He couldn't explain who controlled the two men or who arranged the shipments of the drugs as their role was solely distributing the narcotics and receiving payment. His wife managed the movement of the money and they kept thirty percent for their involvement. Lebrun moved onto the documentation that he had found in the bookcase. He asked what the highlighted colours meant and Gilles squirmed uncomfortably in his seat recalling he'd previously said he didn't know. The detective with Lebrun took the opportunity of a pause in the conversation to acknowledge their appreciation of his cooperation so far reminding him it would be viewed favourably by the court irrespective of the severity of his crime. Vidal turned to his client nodding in recognition of the statement.

Ducourant began again explaining the drugs were shipped within Europe and the highlighters indicated which country was receiving the shipment and also which orders contained drugs or were simply books. In all cases they mixed shipments of narcotics in between shipments that were innocent deliveries of books. He didn't remember the system of colours by heart but he knew that the drug colours were orange, blue and pink. Lebrun acknowledged that the missing colours were green, yellow and brown.

Ducourant nodded and was asked to confirm on tape that these were consignments that contained no drugs.

Gilles Ducourant explained that he and his wife sailed around Europe dropping off the consignments at the various countries. They made deliveries in Paola in southern Italy, Taormina in Sicily and Cala Liberotto in Sardinia. The hotels knew them pretty well by now and they received excellent service. Gilles voice trailed off as he realised that the luxurious holidays were a thing of the past; everything had imploded including his life. Lebrun challenged how they had avoided checks by Customs on entering the ports whilst he privately questioned how this couple could have evaded discovery for so many years. Gilles said they soaked the boxes in lavender oil before repacking them with the tooled books and the copies. The odour emitting from below deck was intense and they only used their cabin, the galley and the upper deck. He and his wife had agreed that they would explain the lavender oil was used to protect the books from termites but they also knew it would create confusion if any Customs Officer boarded with a dog. They sailed in and out of the ports registering their boat on arrival and departure but had rarely needed to accommodate a custom's check which tended to be based on random selection or a tip-off. They had been lucky enough to have had only three random checks. Lebrun and Lepireon registered the information which explained the overpowering lavender oil they'd located at the house.

"And the two mobile phones in your safe were for you to contact the purchasers?" challenged Lepireon. He confirmed they were as his shoulders slumped and his stomach turned to liquid as it dawned on him that the safe had been found. Just for a brief moment he had wondered if he could escape gaol and he and Sophie would still have a decent life on the money in the safe but that dream had been shattered. Lebrun asked when the next "*vacances*" would be taken and Gilles replied "*en trois semaines*" causing the officer to challenge if the highlighted names and addresses on the paperwork were still their holiday destination in three weeks' time. They would need to get Interpol engaged as quickly as possible as the Ducourants' silence over the next few days would ring alarm bells. Gilles Ducourant did not reply but preferred to put his head in his hands and he started to sob. "I need to see my daughter" he declared causing the solicitor to interject and insist the detectives consider the information that his client was offering them. Capitaine Lebrun advised an escorted visit could be arranged but he would need more information plus his signed statement to get the approval required for a visitation. Gilles nodded consent and sighed in relief that he would see Sophie before anyone decided his fate.

"*Monsieur Ducourant, comme votre avocat est présent, je dois retourner à la mort de Jean-Louis Pislait, le connaissiez-vous personnellement?*" demanded the Capitaine. Gilles confirmed that he did not know Jean-Louis as Michel had been the courier of the drugs and his only contact at the boat. "So why were you on the phone to Vialat that morning" continued Serge Lebrun. Gilles started wringing his hands once more before uttering "he had told us about the missing books taken by the British woman and that Pislait was having a crisis of conscience. He was a loose cannon and would have wrecked our successful business relationship. I was trying to work out what to do as Michel had mentioned that he thought he was about to speak to the woman and I didn't know how much he would tell her. I couldn't decide what he should do as I knew they were friends. I didn't get chance to agree a plan as my wife ripped the phone out of my hand". "What was her plan Monsieur Ducourant?" His eyes filled with tears as he responded "she told Michel to stop him immediately and instructed him to kill Pislait". I sensed Michel was refusing but then she told him she'd kill him too and throw him into the Rhône. "I don't think Michel had any choice as it was him or Pislait".

The room fell silent as they absorbed the information. Lepireon knew that they would have extreme difficulty in getting Marie-Noelle Ducourant to agree any liability in Jean-Louis Pislait's death. The level of cooperation in this room compared to her attempts in the room down the corridor was remarkable even with Madame Ducourant now back in a cell awaiting further interview. Lepireon reflected on the woman's repeated "no comment" and changed the line of questioning in the hope of getting some new leverage. "Monsieur Ducourant, did your wife help you deliver the drugs to the various addresses across Europe?" He nodded agreement and Lebrun requested he speak up for the tape. "Yes, we shared getting the parcels to the contacts as we were keen to get the business transactions finished so we could relax on holiday. She had her regulars in the same way that I had mine".

Lebrun noted her involvement in dispersing the packages but it was Lepireon who realised this was a vital link in proving Madame Ducourant's collaboration. She could deny Gilles's statement but they would hopefully get evidence from her mobile phone records and her contacts who would confirm her direct involvement. Gilles Ducourant returned to death of Michel's friend and asked the detectives to confirm he would not be held responsible for the murder as his friend had been placed in an invidious position by his wife. Vidal also looked at the officers awaiting their confirmation. Lebrun said little more on the matter other than his statement would be taken and the facts recorded.

Gilles explained that their last crossing had been horrendous and he'd discussed stopping any future sailings with his wife by suggesting they find another manner of distribution. Marie-Noelle was set against the idea and they'd had yet another row which seemed to be their only method of communication in the last few months. It always fell upon Gilles to weather the storms as she seldom took the wheel leaving him to do the heavy lifting of the route. They had already dropped off a number of the books and were heading back around the tip of Italy on route to Taormina in Sicily having distributed the boxes in a few of the Italian locations. They were coming through the Straits of Messina when a squall arrived with no advance warning. Gilles diligently checked daily weather reports but the area was unpredictable and they were in the middle of it before they could consider a change of route. The squall quickly turned into a major storm and he was forced to take the wheel and remove the autopilot owing to the heavy winds. He had to sail the Skydeck for several hours during the night with only his wife reluctantly providing coffee to keep him awake. The return home had been traumatic and he had spent hours with his wife arguing about the strain of sailing around Europe with the possibility of being searched at every port on their schedule. He would have been happy to modify their lives and invest in the gallery rather than leave Camila to run it single-handedly for the greater part of the year. They listened to his last voyage appreciating he was ready to adapt to a reduced quality of life but his overly demanding wife clearly had other ideas for their future. By the look on the solicitor's face, it was clear he also had a degree of sympathy for his client.

By now the Ducourants had been in the Commisariat for six hours and there was sufficient evidence for them both to be charged and to appear before the courts the next day. Lebrun advised he would arrange for the statement to be typed and that it was important for Gilles Ducourant to read it very carefully and correct any errors which he should make known to the officer present at the time. If he thought it was an accurate reflection of his admission, he would need to sign it as further interviews would be held later following this first cross-examination. Once this was done, he would discuss a visit to see his daughter with his superior. He sincerely hoped that the permission would be granted but the decision was out of his control. He would, however, stress how cooperative Monsieur Ducourant had been during the interview process and Vidal hastily agreed that his client had fully cooperated from the outset. The three officers left the room and a brigadier came in to escort Gilles Ducourant to a cell which was suitably distanced from his wife's.

Lebrun put a call through to Lyon. Capitaine Thierry Barreau listened intently as Serge Lebrun brought him up to speed. He was delighted that such a lengthy drug-running business had been blown wide open and recognised his Interpol colleagues would have their work cut out getting the necessary evidence to convict all of those involved. Barreau updated his colleague on the interviews of the trainees and the trainers at the property outside Lyon. They were all well scripted in explaining the lack of documentation and any incorrect information but they were all guilty of paying or receiving cash payments and Barreau was hopeful that one or two of the ex-convicts might decide a confession was preferable to another term in gaol. Lebrun wished him good luck and asked if he could check some facts with Vialat. Barreau confirmed he was currently in the safe house and would be there until he could arrange his new identity and his transfer out of France. Serge Lebrun needed to know if Vialat had received instruction to kill Pislait from Madame Ducourant or from her husband. He explained Gilles Ducourant's willingness to confess to the various crimes but he was categorically denying any involvement with Pislait's death. Could Thierry check with Vialat whether the instruction to kill Pislait had come from Gilles Ducourant or had it come from his wife. Vialat knew both of them so it should not be a problem to recognise either of their voices. Barreau confirmed he'd get onto it right away and call him within the hour.

Lebrun went to update his Commandant of the progress and alert him of the European connections. The Commandant was aware of the excellent discoveries at Rue des Fabres and listened as his colleague described the confession delivered by Gilles Ducourant. He agreed that he should be kept "on side" as his evidence was critical to the success of the overseas investigations. He agreed for Ducourant to have an accompanied visit to the nursing home to see his daughter. Madame Ducourant should also be given the same opportunity, whether she accepted it or not. They would need to be handcuffed, travel in separate cars and a minimum of two officers would need to be present at all times. The home would have the right to refuse them access if they felt other residents would be affected by the police visit. The Capitaine acknowledged the instructions and confirmed that he would pass the files with the European names and addresses to him as soon as he had duplicates available. He left his senior officer with his cheeks glowing as the plaudits followed him out of the door.

With Gilles Ducourant spilling all, he returned to the office and to Lepireon who was packing up and preparing to return to Avignon. She knew that Lebrun would take charge of interviewing Madame Ducourant so her involvement was potentially coming to a close other than presenting herself in court to support the case at a future date. They had made a great team and she'd really enjoyed working with him and gaining insight into the investigative role. She now questioned whether aspiring to a *Chef de Police Municipale* was still her goal or whether the *Nationale* offered more variety. She would think about the pros and cons on her drive back to Avignon. They shared a winning hug after the conventional three kisses and Lebrun congratulated her again for busting the case open by her discovery of Rue des Fabres. He had not mentioned to her that a report had gone to the Avignon *Chef de Police* to commend her performance and highlight her direct action in solving a narcotics case that had European connections. These actions had also led to a far wider investigation under the control of the Commissariat in Lyon.

Lebrun's day was not over and he asked for Marie-Noelle Ducourant to be brought to interview room SE1. He asked his colleague to join him and they prepared their files and headed to the room. The solicitor hadn't left the station as he'd been forewarned that Capitaine Lebrun would be interviewing Gilles' wife. He opened the interview by asking if she wanted to visit her daughter one last time before being presented in court tomorrow morning. Her hostile and surly expression softened only slightly as she mockingly replied *"je préférerais être au resto Le Petit Palais où nous avions réservé une table à vingt heures. Vous proposez un échange?* Lebrun couldn't hide his shock that a dinner table in a local restaurant would take precedence over a visit to see her daughter. He left the room to inform the brigadiers they would only be taking Monsieur Ducourant to the home and reinforced the Commandant's instructions. It was now late evening and he asked one of his colleagues to ring ahead to alert them. A minimal amount of information should be provided other than it was unlikely his daughter would see him again in the immediate weeks and months.

He returned to the interview room where he repeated that Marie-Noelle Ducourant was held owing to a serious crime at the premises of Rue des Fabres. She would receive a lengthy prison sentence and would leave prison as an elderly lady confined to living out her remaining years. He cautioned her that the sentence might be reduced should she cooperate. She'd heard it all before from the other idiot and opted to laugh in their faces advising they had nothing against her. "Well, on the contrary, we have rather a lot that indicates your active involvement Madame Ducourant" affirmed Serge Lebrun. She spat out "such as?" Capitaine Lebrun confirmed they were aware the drugs were delivered by both of them using the Skydeck yacht. She helped her husband contact the recipients in order they could get the business side of their trip conducted as quickly as possible. At the moment, the overseas Commissariats were in communication with the various people noted on their files and he was sure some of them, if not all, would confirm her mobile phone calls and her presence in passing over the drugs. He knew this was not the case as they had only just received the files but it didn't harm to let her believe they were currently busting the various locations. She didn't flinch at the news and he suspected behind those bright, intelligent eyes, her brain was trying to devise a plan to extricate herself from any involvement.

Lebrun's mobile pinged receipt of a message from Barreau. He read "Vialat a confirmé que c'était Mme Ducourant qui a demandé le meurtre de Pislait. A+. Thierry." Vialat's confirmation that Madame Ducourant had instructed the killing caused Lebrun to declare "this is an extremely serious crime, Madame Ducourant and murder of another human being is reprehensible". "What murder, who's dead?" she proclaimed allowing Lebrun to confirm that her colleague, Michel Vialat, had confirmed that her husband had begun the conversation on the morning of Brother Pislait's death but that she had given the instruction to kill him. She sat upright on the chair proclaiming that the monk acted under his own instruction and she had no involvement. Serge Lebrun confirmed that a court would decide her level of participation but the evidence given by the monk noted that she had instructed Pislait's murder. She would do well to confirm this to them now rather than a court find her guilty.

Marie-Noelle realised this was not going well. Clearly her half-wit husband had vomited every bit of information relating to the trafficking and now he'd stuck her for Pislait's murder. She needed time to think it through but the men in front of her would not stop insisting on replies to questions so she couldn't gather enough time to collect her thoughts and build a defence. She realised Vidal might have helped her but she'd already kicked him out at the start of the interview calling him "*un idiot incompétent*" and had agreed she would defend herself. The ball of string was unravelling faster than her head could stop it. She chose to deny all involvement and returned to the "no comment" response where she felt on safer ground. If she could get back into the cell, maybe there was a chance she could concoct a way out of this mess.

A faltering round of questioning followed before Lebrun, like his Avignon colleague, realised that there was little to be gained from hearing "*je n'ai rien à dire*" response to every question he raised. He chose to return her to the cell and try again after the court hearing; perhaps the reality of appearing in court would loosen her tongue. Lebrun also needed time to consider everything he had heard from Gilles Ducourant and Michel Vialat. The case was strong against the couple but perhaps he could find another way to get a confession from the woman if he slept on the facts.

Whilst Marie-Noelle sat in the cell picking at an unappetising canteen meal whilst fantasising about the Coquilles St Jacques at Le Petit Palais, Gilles was sitting in the back of a police vehicle heading to see his daughter. He asked the officers if he could stop at the florist's shop he had visited since Sophie had been moved from their home at Pointe Rouge. The driver bluntly refused the request but the officer sitting next to him suggested he use his mobile to contact the shop as they might well be closed by now. Fortunately, the owner was still at work preparing bouquets for delivery the next day and he indicated his surprise to hear from Monsieur Ducourant who he'd been expecting throughout the morning. He confirmed his usual order had been prepared and was ready for collection. As they approached the shop, the sympathetic officer rang to alert the owner to come outside with the display and he hurried out staring in disbelief at the sight of the police car. The driver opened the door to accept the flowers and the other officer had taken Gilles' wallet from his pocket and handed over forty euros to the owner. They drove off leaving the florist standing on the kerb open-mouthed in astonishment. As expected, the nursing home personnel were equally shocked to see Gilles Ducourant arrive with a police escort and even more horrified and distressed to see he was wearing handcuffs. The Deputy Manager recommended the cuffs be removed before going to Sophie's room, however, the police officers apologised and confirmed they were a condition of the visit. There was nothing to be done and Gilles Ducourant cut across their apologies to advise he just wanted to see his daughter.

They went up to the room where she was in bed and awake. The staff had confirmed that her father was coming to see her so she'd stopped hitting her head against the furniture and had even eaten half of her supper. Gilles wanted to cuddle her in his arms but the constraints blocked him. Sophie looked at her father and pointed to the handcuffs "*Dada es-tu un policier?*" she chuckled and her father agreed "*Oui, aujourd'hui je suis un policier. Regardes, chouchou, j'ai des amis avec moi*". His daughter clapped her hands and laughed as she acknowledged her father's two police friends who stood uncomfortably by the bedroom door and next to the window. The officer near the window affectionately waved his hand until his colleague barked "Brigadier Vertaure" and he threw his hand down to his side and adopted a repentant stance. As Gilles was shackled, he asked the driver if he would remove the dead flowers on a table in the corner of the room and replace them with the fresh ones. This led to a few expletives and Gilles caught words like "*entrer police*" and "*arrangeur floral*". The driver did a passable job and, once more, the room was full of pink, yellow and orange blooms; Sophie's favourite colours. Gilles did his best to stroke her hair and she hauled herself up to try and hug him. She had huge difficulty controlling her movements and Gilles knew the pain this gesture would induce in her. She whimpered but managed to get her arms around his neck and give him a kiss that was aimed at his cheek but ended up on his ear.

He hooked his arms over her head and the two of them held each other until the pain wracked through Sophie and she told her father to stop. Gilles' eyes were full of tears and even the two officers were shifting awkwardly sensing the emotion in the room. Gilles instructed his daughter to be *"un ange pour son papa et des infirmières"* adding under his breath that he might not visit for a long time. Sophie didn't fully understand why he was saying she should be an angel for him and the nurses but her father seemed to be crying so this was making her cry too. He kissed her one more time and looked across at the officers acknowledging it was time to go. They left the room to Sophie's grunts and shouts of *"Dada? Reviens, reviens s'il te plaît"* and one of the officers took Gilles Ducourant's arm in case his sobbing caused him to fall down the staircase. They didn't know what he was accused of, or whether he was guilty of it, but they did wonder whether it was worth all the pain he was currently experiencing. His handicapped daughter clearly adored him and he adored her in return. Two lives had been ravaged by whatever he had done. Sometimes Brigadier Vertaure hated his job and he looked across at his dispassionate colleague who also looked equally dejected.

At the court hearing the next day, the couple were retained for only for a few minutes as they acknowledged their names and home address and listened to a definition of their crimes. Afterwards they were taken to the local prison at Baumette where Lebrun opted to speak to Madame Ducourant in the hope she would have witnessed sufficient discomfort that she might be more agreeable and forthcoming with information. Unfortunately, it was not the case as he was confronted with an irritable woman who unequivocally refused to cooperate, just as she had done at the police station. He confirmed they were currently building the case against her and her husband, he had evidence that she had instructed the murder of Jean-Louis Pislait and that he would see her back in court. She turned her back on him like a petulant child and Lebrun laughed out loud as he stepped out of the interview room and walked down to the corridor to the security gates.

CHAPTER THIRTEEN
NORMAL SERVICE RESUMED

Lottie was enjoying a return to normal life at the *brocante*. Another television company had decided to use the emporium items for their production and Francine had taken a call from a local theatre group. Everything was bright and encouraging in her world including her relationship with Philippe who she now accepted was a huge comfort and important to her. She looked forward to his messages and going for a drink after work or sharing a restaurant meal. She had shared a few kisses with him which were much more than a peck on the cheek and she began to talk more openly about him with the children and her friends. Mimi was delighted to hear that she was dating Philippe causing Lottie to rebuff the remark and advise it was not "dating". "*Donc, c'est quoi précisement, ma chère?*" She tried to respond that women of fifty-six years of age don't date any more like smitten teenagers but then realised that it was a nonsense preferring to agree with her friend.

She hadn't seen Cédric for a few days and so decided to pop over and see him on Friday morning. She enjoyed their chats which he clearly relished given she usually stored up a bits of local news to share with him. He was already out in the garden at eleven o'clock and Lottie suggested they share a couple of eclairs with a cup of coffee. She said she go and make the drinks but he preferred to go with her to the room as he had something to show her. She wondered if it would be an item he had repaired for a resident as he usually had one or two trinkets on his desk alongside a selection of tools. She put the kettle on and got two plates from the cupboard. Cédric presented her with a small blue notebook beautifully bound in a leather tooled cover. Inside the book was a list of dates, book titles, flight numbers, shipping references, and prices. Lottie was dumbfounded by the little notebook and queried "is this what I think it is? A list of every shipment you received from your nephew and then Michel Vialat?" Cédric confirmed it was and he hadn't thought to give it to her before because he feared that there would still be consignments coming to him. Nothing had appeared during the last three weeks and the dealers knew the police were tracking them so maybe it was the right time to hand it to the authorities?

It didn't surprise her that this conscientious and detailed man had written down every consignment since the moment he had received them. He'd been flawlessly meticulous when she first met him. Maybe it would be impossible for the police to know which deliveries contained drugs but, even so, this factual tracking of the consignments must surely be gold dust. She kissed him on the cheek and said it would be very helpful for the police to have such a comprehensive record of the consignments. She put the book in her handbag to pass to "worst case". She turned to make the coffee and passed one of the coffee eclairs to Cédric who rubbed his hands together like a small child and exclaimed "*Youpi!*"

They chatted on about nothing in particular and shared a game of Scrabble in a hysterical mix of French and English words which made the game much easier given the additional flexibility. She stayed until the lunch was delivered and promised to see him in the next couple of weeks. She would pass the notebook to "worst case" and Cédric snickered at Lottie's pet name for her and the humorous translation.

She was rather excited at the opportunity to talk to Lepireon again as she had no idea how their enquiries were progressing. Had they caught the man who had killed Jean-Louis and had they identified the people involved in the cocaine shipments? When she got home, she put a call through to her. She was delighted to find the Brigadier-Chef in the Avignon office and to learn she had recently returned after a number of days in Marseille related to the case. Lottie explained the notebook and Lepireon acknowledged it would be extremely helpful and she could either collect it this afternoon or Madame Pearce could deliver it to the office. Lottie preferred that she collected it as she hoped to quiz her whilst she was out of the office environment.

The doorbell rang just before Lottie was about to start preparing dinner and she buzzed in Brigadier-Chef Lepireon and stepped out to meet her in the corridor. They shook hands warmly and acknowledged it had been a little while since they'd had reason to be in touch. Lottie invited her into the apartment and handed over the notebook which "worst case" opened and smiled at the detailed lists in front of her. *"C'est inestimable, Madame Pearce. Veuillez remercier Monsieur Mallet de sa diligence, s'il vous plaît"*. Lottie confirmed that she would pass on the policewoman's thanks for his detailed records and then probed for more details on the case and if they had caught Jean-Louis' killer. Lepireon acknowledged that they were holding two people in custody for trafficking narcotics and the murder of Brother Pislait. She was not able to disclose further information, however, the support of Madame Pearce and Monsieur Mallet had been instrumental in bringing the people to count. Lottie lobbed further questions at the woman realising it was unlikely she'd get any further details from her which proved to be the case. She was happy someone would be sentenced with the man's death and confirmed she would update Monsieur Mallet. She knew he'd be equally delighted that his nephew's death was not in vain and that the drug operation was now under investigation with two people in custody. "Worst case" asked after the *brocante* and if Madame Pearce was enjoying her new business and her life in France. Lottie confirmed that she was blissfully content and the only negative aspect was her family who were so far away. She was a grandmother again and it was a huge wrench to be separated from her new granddaughter. "Worst case" acknowledged that family were important and maybe she would have time to fly back from Avignon or Nimes in the coming weeks. They shook hands once more and Lepireon headed home to her own family.

Lottie was in the office on Monday when the postman arrived. She was surprised to see an envelope embossed with "*Commissariat de Police de Lyon*". That was astonishing and confusing in itself but it contained a further envelope marked "*L'Abbaye de Notre Croix de Fer*". She thought of the monk chasing Jean-Louis and opened it with a sense of trepidation. Her eyes dropped to the bottom where she noted the letter was written by the abbot. It was handwritten and in a beautiful copperplate which made it complicated to read and translate. It was addressed "au sauveur de notre abbaye" or "to the saviour of our abbey". The abbot confirmed that a Lyon detective was currently investigating a malicious group of men who were masquerading as monks and were focused on crime or stealing the treasures in France's abbeys. He had fallen foul of these people here at *L'Abbaye de Notre Croix de Fer* and was thankful they had been identified and removed from his family. He was shocked and hurt that a close friend had been a part of the operation and the abbey and the monks were now focused on healing and repairing the breach of trust. He was unclear of the precise details but he had insisted that the Lyon Commissariat allow him to thank the person involved in expunging the cankers in their small family. The Lyon Commissariat had suggested he write a letter which they would pass to the person involved. It ended with his renewed thanks and Lottie held it to her chest as if it would disintegrate at any moment.

She put the beautiful letter in her bag to show Cédric at her next visit and returned to the rest of the post. There was a letter from a television company confirming a designer, his assistant and a prop buyer would visit the emporium before the end of the week to select items for a one-off drama. This day couldn't get any better as she scampered off to the workshop to check the new stock Claude had located over the weekend. She couldn't wait for next week when she had her very first visitor to her home in Avignon. If it couldn't be Lou, Ali or Thomas then the next best visitor would most certainly be her mate, Jill, who would be visiting for three days.

Claude and Francine had agreed to cover her days at the brocante so she'd be free to show her friend around Avignon and the other delights offered throughout the region. She'd already selected a few day trips in her mind and the first day would retrace the lovely afternoon she'd spent with Mimi in St-Rémy-de-Provence and then onto Isle-sur-La- Sorgue. Such a lot had happened to her life since that serendipitous day visiting Bob's teenage friend. She hardly recognised the woman who'd apprehensively sat at her laptop in trepidation at the thought of writing to some woman called Mireille Rivaud who was the mother of Bob's first child. Even Marlow and its bubbling, busy High Street stretched her imagination as she compared it to the Avignon's city centre; the only thing in common was a river that ran alongside the town and this city.

On her way home, she popped into the newsagent and picked up a copy of the Midi-Libre; the daily, regional newspaper which Lottie bought from time to time to help improve her vocabulary. Initially, reading the newspaper had proved a chore as she'd underlined the words she didn't know and looked them up in a dictionary. Now she congratulated herself that she could read the articles with only a smattering of words to be checked and these tended to be idioms. She'd invested in an enormous dictionary which was worth the investment as many of the expressions were noted under the key word. She poured herself a glass of rosé and sat down to scan the paper before arranging her supper.

On the front page was a photo of a building somewhere near Lyon and underneath it were the words "The company's residential training centre". She was about to turn the page when she spotted the words "Jean-Louis Pislait" and turned back to read the article in more detail. It noted the recent court hearing of Gilles Ducourant and Marie-Noelle Ducourant, a husband-and-wife team who had been found guilty of trafficking narcotics. The combined police forces of Avignon, Marseille and Lyon had been instrumental in toppling their distribution of cocaine which had been operating for six years and had involved several countries across Europe. Gilles Ducourant had been found guilty and received a twenty-year prison term whilst his wife had received a life sentence owing to her direct involvement in the murder of Jean-Louis Pislait, a religious brother living at an abbey located near Lyon. A second investigation, under the authority of the Lyon Commisariat, had led to the investigation of a corrupt group operating as monks who infiltrated abbeys throughout France. The leader of this group, Georges Léa, was currently being held in Corbas prison awaiting trial.

Lottie realised that this couple must have been the people that Lepireon had mentioned a few months ago. The trial had taken weeks to build the evidence but it had started with her buying those damn books. She slurped the remains of her glass and put the newspaper aside to take to Cédric. A life sentence for the woman who had killed his nephew; she hoped he would take comfort from the verdict and wondered if she should ring him tonight or wait until Jill had left and pop over to see him. She decided that it might be better to be present when he read the article and opted to wait.

She was so excited at the thought of Jill's arrival and was checking the weather forecast every day as the kids were always envious of her descriptions of it being too hot or how the azure blue skies were totally without clouds. She was feeling a bit sick that the weather might take a sudden nosedive before Jill arrived and she'd go home disappointed. Her fingers were firmly crossed that they wouldn't have to suffer a stint of the Mistral wind which arrived with little notice and could seriously impact sight-seeing. It was the end of the tourist season so the other worry would be the storms as Mimi had explained the break in the hot weather could cause huge storms with thunder and lightning. These were accompanied by torrential downpours that hit the hard-baked ground and could easily create flash floods. The *brocante* and its roof were sound during these alarming periods but Alain would need to keep an eye on the despatch area as water could back up into the workshop.

She knew that Jill had not visited the area before so she hoped her loosely planned itinerary would suit her dear friend. The break included an invitation for Philippe to join her and Jill at the restaurant with the olive tree on Sunday evening. She'd been back a few times as it was a good fifteen minutes' walk from the apartment and she could enjoy a glass of wine or two and walk it off going home. He'd jumped at the idea as he realised she'd be busy with her friend in the coming days and he wouldn't see so much of her. He'd become rather used to having Lottie in his life and even his daughter was a huge fan which was fortuitous since Nat had only met her once at dinner and once for coffee on a Saturday morning. Jill didn't know about the dinner reservation as Lottie wanted it to be a surprise so she could quiz her later as to whether he was a good match for her. Lottie was suppressing her feelings but she knew that her earlier concerns for Bob and her family were being replaced by a need to have love, tenderness and also intimacy back in her life. These pleasures would have been hard to renew back in Marlow but the distance, together with her recreating a new life in France, gave her the reassurance that she needed to take her relationship with Philippe to the next stage.

It was the end of the season but there were still flights from the UK coming into Avignon airport. Jill's visit just fitted inside the current schedule before the winter timetable made the local airport unavailable to both of them. Lottie was still relatively spoilt with airports as there were two locally in Avignon and Nimes and even the airports of Montpellier and Marseille, which were only an hour's drive away, were easily accessible. She was yearning for a good natter with her friend as the endless Skype calls or WhatsApp messages just didn't hit the same spot as sitting down with a bottle of wine and having a damn good chinwag with her mate. She drove to the airport and parked up early as if she might hasten the plane's arrival and avoid a good twenty minutes' wait. She searched the sea of faces in the "Arrivals" area of the hall until she eventually spotted her amid the herd; there she was waving uncontrollably at her friend clipping the sunglasses off the head of a French Adonis resulting in a string of abuse. They fell into hysterics and a confused muddle of hugs and kisses as Lottie relieved her of the black suitcase enquiring after the flight and the ghastly early start. The Renault Estate was soon sweeping into the apartment driveway to the delight of her friend who had to be reminded that it was a rented apartment within the building. "I don't care, it's bloody lovely Lots" she declared.

Jill set her case in the spare room and unpacked the handful of clothes and gave Lottie a huge plastic bag loaded with teabags. The French loved their Liptons tea but it was weaker affair and drunk without milk so she found it no substitute to a good old cup of PG Tips. Once refreshed, they set off to St Remy where they enjoyed a three-course lunch which began with Rillettes de porc with cornichons and the rusk-like biscottes, follow by a Lapin à la Cocotte with braised chicory and finished off with a little fluted bowl of mocha mousse with a langue de chat sugary biscuit. As Jill wiped her mouth on the napkin, she declared "that was divine, where's the bed for a lie-down?" Lottie laughed admitting that she rarely ate out so she too was bursting at the seams. "We'll walk it off as why don't we have a stroll around Glanum, have you heard of it Jill?" She confirmed that she hadn't so Lottie provided a brief history advising it dated back to pre-Roman times but was known for the remaining structures of the Roman period dating back to the seventh century. There were several tourist boards, in French and English, strategically placed throughout the site so they could read about the edifices whilst enjoying a gentle stroll to work off their lunch. It was one of those riveting locations where you felt like you had a virtual reality headset clamped on your skull as you imagined the daily lives of the Romans living in the city. They spent a little time studying the replica model in the entrance hall so that they had an idea of the layout of the site before stepping back out into the warm, late summer afternoon.

It was no surprise that Jill loved the archaic setting as she strolled under the arch taking photos of the decorated stone panels and crawled over the rocky stones of the residential quarters and the public baths; her camera clicking incessantly.

Once they'd left the ruins of Glanum, they fell into the car and headed off towards the water wheels of Isle-sur-la-Sorgue. Lottie explained that they were retracing old steps of her arrival in France when she'd first met Mimi even though she'd discovered many other wonderful towns and villages since her arrival. If Jill was up for it, they would go to the open-air market in Uzès tomorrow followed by a picnic lunch at the Pont du Gard. "Too right I'm up for it Lots. As you know, I love a French market and the weather's great for outdoor eating. It all sounds fab, I'm happy just sharing some time with you". Lottie smiled and hugged her friend as they strolled along the small river running through the town. Lottie explained that every

Sunday, the streets were transformed into one giant antique market and she often came here to negotiate a price on selected gems. They weaved along the lanes stopping only for a glass of chilled pale pink rosé in a riverside café liberally adorned with sky-blue plumbago. "Dinner at home tonight as you must be knackered after your early start" Lottie declared to her sagging friend. The combination of the early start plus wine at lunchtime and now the glasses of rosé were causing them both to wilt. Jill readily consented to the plan as Lottie went to find the waiter so she could pay the bill.

As Lottie threw together a pasta meal, Jill showered and phoned her husband to describe her inaugural afternoon in the South of France. Lottie couldn't help but overhear as she recounted the beauty of the light in the region and how it created a golden glow on the limestone buildings. Lottie realised how quickly she had accepted these beautiful aspects as the "norm" and listened with fresh ears and a warm heart as she realised these beauties were her home. Jill was telling Martin how she now understood why so many famous artists had selected the region to capture its beauty in oils. She had her camera on charge to ensure she was fully prepared for tomorrow's treasures, be they the folk bustling around in the market or the World Heritage aqueduct. Lottie stuck her head around the bedroom door gesturing that the pasta was ready so Jill signed off with her hubby and went into the kitchen to find two bowls of steaming crab linguine and a bottle of white wine emerging from a glass ice bucket overflowing with ice cubes.

After a deep sleep no doubt aided by alcohol, they both awoke early in readiness for the trip to the market. Lottie had already been up an hour and had prepared the picnic as they'd both agreed to have breakfast in Uzès rather than delay the chance of finding a parking spot. Lottie had learned from the locals that many of the previous rough terrains which had proved useful parking for the Producers' market on Wednesdays and the huge Saturday markets had been sold to developers. The result was a collection of huge monoliths of holiday apartments which created a serious lack of parking. It was not uncommon for the traffic to gridlock as the early birds, who arrived at eight o'clock, made way for the sleepy latecomers. The early hour ensured they easily found an available spot in the car park behind *La Poste*. They headed off to the café "*La Nougatine*" which Lottie knew would be heaving with locals and tourists all demanding a croissant and café crème. The walk from the car park gave Jill the chance to photograph an accordion player leaning against the wall who gave her an exaggerated wink in the hope of a few coins in his grubby hat. Like many other visitors before her, she felt that taking his photo deserved a reward so she dropped fifty centimes into the makeshift bag as he blew her a kiss in acknowledgement.

After breakfast, Jill and Lottie bought a couple of tasty tartlets from the café for their picnic dessert and made their way into the central market feature of the Place Aux Herbes. As they fought through the bustling mixture of locals and sightseers, both had to take care not to step on the paws of small dogs or knock a small toddler's hand from the safeguard of their parent's control. Lottie purchased fresh olives with espelette to add to their alfresco lunch as Jill clicked away with her camera busily capturing shots of the French artisans; most of which were desperately trying to sell their wares as they spotted the real buyers amid the mass of humanity. Two hours had disappeared strolling through the streets following the market stalls before they both headed to the car park and onto the Pont du Gard.

Lottie suggested pitching their folding chairs on a flattened area under a wizened olive tree that would provide some shade from the midday sun which Jill was loving but Lottie was hoping to avoid. This gave them a spectacular view overlooking the Roman aqueduct and Lottie suggested Jill take some photos whilst she laid out the picnic spread. Her friend was only too happy to agree as she headed off to the walkway along the bridge bending down to run her hand through the bushes of wild rosemary. Lottie sorted the picnic bag to locate the market olives and the sliced walnut and pork *saucisson* to munch as an aperitif with their chilled Costière de Nîmes white wine. She sorted the remaining picnic boxes so as they could seamlessly move through the courses and beckoned to Jill after fifteen minutes of watching her friend point and click her camera at everything that moved.

They sat in silence enjoying their favourite pastime of people watching as they picked at the olives and slurped from their plastic glasses. It was no surprise that the conversations of many people passing them were in an assortment of French, German, Dutch, English, and Scandinavian. They exchanged raised eyebrows at a giggling group of petite Asian girls as they perfected their poses, smoothed their hair and pointed their toes in an exaggerated fashion as they took their selfies. "I've died and gone to heaven" exclaimed Jill. "I totally get why you're so happy here. I'm so proud of you as losing Bob could have easily been a reason to stay in a safe situation in Marlow but you threw caution to the wind and not only changed country but also invested in a new business. I'm so happy it's all worked out". Lottie agreed with her friend that it had been a huge risk but the signs were encouraging that the business would thrive, however, the only downside was the distance from her family and friends. During the many Skype calls, she'd already shared with her the problem of the cocaine books, the involvement with the police and the horrendous death in Avignon. These events had naturally horrified Jill who subsequently messaged on a regular basis to check Lottie was safe; she had even phoned Lou to discuss the level of danger that might be circling her dear friend. It was a huge relief once she knew the police had taken ownership of the case and her friend was no longer exposed to life-threatening events. She couldn't imagine drug trafficking affecting Lottie in the charity shop or in Barbara's antique business.

They sat under the olive tree exchanging memories of the past and revisiting some of the recent conversations via Skype and WhatsApp. The picnic was long finished and it was only the flies and one or two wasps that caused them to fold away the chairs, load the picnic bag and head to the car park once more. "I enjoy speaking French but you've no idea how great it is to just natter on in English Jill" Lottie declared. "Sometimes it's so hard to convey the subtleties or nuances of the English language and to try and do that in French is impossible. I'm loving the freedom of just talking to you without searching for words every couple of seconds!" Jill understood the problem as she had such a limited understanding of the language that she couldn't imagine how her friend coped when it was nonstop.

In no time at all, the moment of Jill's final evening was upon them promising the night out at the restaurant with Philippe. Jill had referenced him several times during her stay causing Lottie to admit that she would meet him just before she left. Jill was delighted as she wanted to ensure he was a worthy companion for her friend who was finding her feet after Bob's sudden death. Everything she'd heard about him so far was encouraging but to actually meet him in person was even better. At the restaurant, she found she wasn't disappointed as she could see exactly why Lottie was attracted to him. He not only looked great for his years but he had a warm, open manner and clearly adored Lottie. His broken English with a French accent was a total winner in Jill's eyes and, yet again, she found herself slightly envying her mate and her decision to take the plunge on moving to France. As they walked home, she reassured Lottie that he was an excellent partner and she could easily understand how she had fallen for him as they really complimented each other. She had felt like a friend from the minute she'd met him which was odd given the only link between them was Lottie but it spoke volumes of his character; he mostly definitely had her seal of approval. Lottie stopped walking and hugged her friend in delight. "That means so much to me Jill. I've been worrying if it's all too quick and whether I'm rushing into a fresh start or running away from grief. Thank you for being honest; you're a true friend".

Lottie was deeply saddened at Jill's departure the next morning. They made promises of Lottie going to Marlow for Christmas and Jill had an open invitation to return, with or without Martin, and yet nothing could fill the gap in Lottie's happiness as she drove back to the apartment. She stripped the bed, put the washing machine on and made a coffee as she attempted to find the rhythm of life before Jill's visit. She rang Francine to catch up on events at the brocante and her mood changed with news that seven of her items had been sold to an elderly couple setting up a new home for their niece.

She told herself that it was only natural to feel sadness when family and friends returned to the UK. It was logical to miss speaking in English and having to communicate in

French. This new, uncomfortable emotion stayed with her for a couple of days until she found herself adapting again to her Mediterranean lifestyle. Maybe visits from family and friends were yet another learning curve in this adventure?

CHAPTER FOURTEEN
OVERSEAS CONNECTION

As Lottie arrived at the brocante after Jill's visit, much further afield, in another continent, sat a middle-aged man also embarking on a new life.

Sitting in his comfortable townhouse in Quebec, Michel Vialat, or Roger Coursat as he was now known, reflected on his new identity created for his life in Canada where he awaited the forthcoming court case and his evidence which would be given in two weeks' time via video link. He had already supplied and signed a written confession of his role in the drug-trafficking, however, he'd been advised to expect a video link now the case was scheduled at the end of the month. He was relieved to hear that his friend's murder had been rightly attributed to Marie-Noelle and not to his friend Gilles. She had always been the threatening and combative one in the relationship even if she had masterminded the successful narcotics empire and created the sarabaite operation with her brother. It was no surprise to Vialat that the sarabaites' links had brought them all together nor that the successful partnership was now in such a mess. Marie-Noelle and Gilles had been overly ambitious in preserving their excessive lifestyles and this greed had pushed them all off the cliff. He reflected that at least he could still walk down the street plus he'd be bottling his own wine in a few months whilst the Ducourants' future was unlikely to look so bright.

Roger Coursat had easily settled in his new, cheerful home which needed little done to it in terms of restoration or repair. The current owner had even left some of the larger furniture which was a blessing given he'd arrived with nothing. He'd managed to equip most of the missing furniture or culinary tools from a local store when he'd reached out for items that were provided by the abbey but non-existent in his current home. It had been hard to take on a totally new identity and move away from his beloved France and yet he knew that he would never be safe there; particularly once he had given evidence against the sarabaites and the Ducourants. He knew nobody in Quebec and he kept himself very much to himself and yet he was not lonely. The time at the abbey had taught him how to enjoy his own company and be thankful for the simple pleasures in life. He thought of his years amongst the warm brotherhood and of his gradual increase in responsibility at the abbey. He hoped the abbot would delve deep in his soul to forgive him as the French police had advised against him writing to explain his actions. He held treasured memories of his time at *L'Abbaye de Notre Croix de Fer* which only paled when he thought of Jean-Louis whose agonised face never left him when he reflected on the moment he'd pushed him under the wheels of the truck.

He turned his thoughts to the forthcoming purchase of five fields of vines just a few kilometres outside of the city. His early years had been spent helping his father on a vineyard producing the excellent northern Rhône white wine known as Condrieu so he was no stranger to the role and the only difference would be the variety of grapes given Quebec's harsh winters. He had purchased a few acres of seyval blanc vines which were a much hardier variety and produced a hugely popular wine which was mostly consumed across Canada rather than exported. He'd need to think about employing some staff for the fields before the signature date and he'd already put the word out for a cavist as this could take some time. The seller had given him his client list which included local supermarkets so he'd already been in touch with the managers to ensure his distribution would be guaranteed. Yes, life was looking up and he just needed the agent to deliver a copy of the final sales document so he could ensure his first harvest would be available for his clients. He was pleased to witness the current owner was still maintaining the vines as it would have been so easy to sign the *Compromis de Vente* and then step back and let them go to ruin. He was out amid the vines in all weathers pruning them, rewiring the rows and ensuring everything was ready for next year and the new owner. He had been given a half dozen bottles of different vintages and he'd thoroughly enjoyed all of them. He looked forward to producing a similar quality and maybe expanding his client base.

He received a call from the estate agent to advise he'd send a colleague over with the sales contract for the vines. He'd need to check the details and sign it whilst Louis was still with him. The agency could then arrange a date with the solicitor to finalise the purchase. Roger Coursat confirmed that he would be home all day and would read and sign the contract and ensure he gave it back to the employee. He was replacing a light bulb in the hallway when a car pulled into the driveway causing him to instinctively to go on the defensive until he remembered the agency visit.

A young lad jumped out of a rather scruffy vehicle in jeans, check shirt and the obligatory baseball cap. They shook hands and Roger explained he was expecting him as they walked into the sitting room. He suggested a cup of coffee which the lad eagerly accepted causing Roger to head off to the kitchen to put the kettle on and arrange two mugs on a tray. "How long have you worked for the agency?" he shouted through to the sitting room and the young man replied "about six months". He added that he was hoping to be promoted to a sales agent in a couple of months as how hard could selling houses be if you were a wheeler dealer? Roger Coursat was considering the man's arrogant remark when he heard him enter the kitchen. Something was out of kilter with his observation so far of the professional estate agency and he was wondering whether he should give Thomas, the agent managing his deal, some feedback about this guy.

Perhaps he should have known better and not doubted the sarabaites' ability to track him down but he truly believed he was safe so he had no warning as a hyperdermic syringe was driven into his left arm. He stared at the smirking young lad in both shock and horror as he slumped into the kitchen unit reaching out for the carving knife in the sink. He thought of Jean-Louis, his father and mother, the abbot and his promising new start in Quebec before the lights finally went out and the knife tumbled back into the stainless-steel basin. He didn't even hear the kid exclaim "a present for you Brother Vialat" as he calmly checked for a pulse, accepted there was none, then sent a text message before calmly wrapping the syringe in a cloth and putting it back in his jacket pocket. After wiping down the doorbell and Vialat's right hand, he jumped back into his grubby car and considered he might now have the funds for an upgrade.

There was little coverage of the death of Roger Coursat. The local paper reported "Sudden death of a newcomer to Quebec from mainland France". The main article explained that Monsieur Coursat had recently moved into the area and was due to purchase various parcels of land with which to grow seyval blanc grapes. The reporter believed that Monsieur Coursat had been unaware of a heart condition and had, unfortunately, suffered a severe heart attack and been found dead by an estate agent visiting the house some hours later. Monsieur Coursat had no known family in Canada or in France and his death was not being treated as suspicious. The newspaper article was extremely brief and tucked away on page five although no one reading it that morning would have known that the truth had been suppressed by the city Police Station. There was no reference to the evidence from the autopsy, the discovery of the needle entry or the substance in his bloodstream. The only people who received the coroner's report were the Quebec Police Station who forwarded it onto two recipients in France: Capitaine Serge Lebrun at the Marseille Commisariat and CapitaineThierry Barreau based in Lyon.

There was no reason a man's heart attack on the other side of the world would get any coverage in the French national newspapers, let alone the local ones, therefore Lottie would never learn of the demise of Brother Michel Vialat. If she had read of his death, maybe she would have considered it justice or karma for the man who had killed his friend. She would have been able to tell Cédric that justice had come full circle for his nephew's murder and not questioned herself whether events might have been very different if she'd allowed Jean-Louis to talk to her that morning in Rue de la République.

Without doubt the early months in France had been dangerous and terrifying following the chance purchase of those beautiful, tooled leather books. She'd been dragged unwittingly into the world of narcotics, murder and drug distribution. Somehow, along this horrific road, she had developed a relationship with Philippe and had leant on him more and more as the feelings and emotions had developed between them. Would her next adventure be a romantic one? She was definitely ready and she had no doubt that Philippe was ready too.

COMING SOON by the same author:

THE ADVENTURES OF LOTTIE: The Syndicate

The second book in the murder mystery series by author, Gill Meredith. Following on from her adventure in "Not All Bookworms Read", Lottie falls back into the routine of running the brocante in Avignon until the day she discovers a knife in one of the cushions recently hired to a theatre company. She becomes an unwitting player in the murder of a renowned actor at a local theatre whilst, south of Grasse, the mutilated body parts of a young lad from Cannes have been found in the River Siagne.

Once more the English woman finds herself drawn into murder and suspense as both crimes hits the headlines. Will anyone find the link that connects these events or will the culprits evade justice?

by the same author ……

MA CRÊPE SUZETTE: A Life in France

A "must read" for anyone dreaming of moving to France to avoid the rat race. The book opens with a leisurely introduction of how Gill became a Francophile, purchased a holiday home and decided to leave the power jobs behind her. It covers the highs and lows of her Property Management business, her dealings with French bureaucrats and the joys of working in the South of France.

This book will transport you to the region of Occitanie (formerly Languedoc Roussillon) where you will smell the wild rosemary and lavender, feel the Mistral wind and visualise the distinctive bright colours celebrated by owners and tourists alike. Follow Gill's transformation from quintessential business suit and high heels to shorts, polo shirt and espadrilles.

by the same author ......

HOW TO BE A PROPERTY MANAGER: South of France

The role of a Property Manager is a varied one. It can be the management and administration of a collection of properties in a development, managing holiday homes in various parts of the world, or simply helping a neighbour with a weekend holiday home next door. The person fitting the role could be someone operating a business with a high degree of responsibility through to a key holder for emergencies. This guide is aimed at the former and the role of a Property Manager looking after holiday homes in the South of France. If you want to be a Property Manager elsewhere, you will still find valuable advice and information despite a different nationality, culture and environment.

There are sample documents, tips on handling bureaucrats, how to create a business, and the day-to-day role. Many of the properties were rented out as a source of income, therefore, details are provided on how to manage rentals and the associated documentation. There is also a chapter on selling and buying homes for anyone seeking their place in the sun.

You will find a wide selection of real stories that occurred at the many properties and these are interspersed with practical advice. The Property Manager wears many hats!

Printed in Poland
by Amazon Fulfillment
Poland Sp. z o.o., Wrocław

80990715R00132